# A Matter of Souls

# A Matter of Souls

Denise Lewis Patrick

carolrhoda LAB
MINNEAPOLIS

Carolrhoda Lab™
An imprint of Carolrhoda Books
A division of Lerner Publishing Group, Inc.
241 First Avenue North
Minneapolis, MN 55401 U.S.A.

For reading levels and more information, look up this title at www.lernerbooks.com



Main body text set in Janson Text LT Std 10/14.
Typeface provided by Linotype AG.

Library of Congress Cataloging-in-Publication Data

Patrick, Denise Lewis.
A matter of souls / Denise Lewis Patrick.
pages cm
Summary: A series of vignettes reveal life in the Deep South for African Americans as they experience discrimination in a doctor's office, lynching, and other forms of oppression, especially during the 1960s.
ISBN 978-0-7613-9280-4 (trade hard cover : alk. paper)
ISBN 978-1-4677-2402-9 (eBook)
[1. Race relations—Fiction. 2. African Americans—Southern States—Fiction. 3. Southern States—History—Fiction.] I. Title.
PZ7.P2747Mat 2014
[Fic]—dc23 2013017597

Manufactured in the United States of America
1 – BP – 12/31/13

For My Father

## Contents

# The Colored Waiting Room

Elsie Timmons had gone through the wrong door. Maybe it was a mistake. All she knew was that her mama, Luther Mae, was hollering at the top of her lungs for her to "Bring her womanish behind back, right now!"

In fact, there didn't seem to be any other sounds at all on that late summer day in front of Dr. Baker's neat brick office building. Just the strange, trumpeting tone of Luther Mae Timmons's words.

"Girl, I *said* come back here!" Elsie had to turn around. Her mama's voice sounded shaky, that way it always did when Papa brought her a tiny sack of peppermints along with his paycheck, or when that big black phone would ring and she'd sit down hard, because somebody—some cousin or aunt, or uncle's first wife—had died.

Elsie had to shade her eyes; fall hadn't set in deep enough yet to dull the brightness of the Southern sun. As the automatic glass door began to shut, Elsie could see her mother out there, slapping her thigh in frustration . . . no, it was fear! The navy pleats fanned in and out at each strike, and Elsie imagined the nasty red welts that must be rising on her mother's Carnation-milk skin. Elsie put her brown hand on the door handle. She was torn, and just a little bit worried.

But before she eased her mother's mind, before she let herself go back to being the "sweet, levelheaded child" that everybody at Galilee Baptist said she was, she had to *see*.

Her heart fell, and her face must have fallen a little, too. The White waiting room was near about empty, with only a very skinny man in a corner chair. He was staring at a piece of paper that he held in his hands. Elsie guessed that he must be hard of hearing, or shortsighted, or both—because he didn't even flinch when she stepped in. She glanced around, looking for something—she didn't know what. There were rows of armchairs; there was a potted plant; and a low coffee table held an arrangement of magazines. The sliding, frosted glass office window was closed.

Elsie's civil rights experiment had failed. Her mother was the only one worked up sufficiently—and Elsie felt sorry for that.

She banged the door open and stepped back out into the heat.

"Oh Lord, girl! What'd they say? You gonna give me a heart attack one day. You all right? 'Cause—"

"Mama." Elsie allowed herself to be womanhandled, every bone and joint checked, as if she'd just come back from the war. Her brother was there, there in Vietnam, and he would get the same when he came back, didn't matter that he was twenty-two. If he came back.

"Mama, there wasn't nobody in there. I'm fine."

Luther Mae sighed and straightened herself. Suddenly her backbone was like a board, and the way she held her head, the flush on her cheeks looked exactly like a hint of red rouge. The oil on her chocolate-brown waves glistened, and Elsie was reminded of a movie star in one of the double features at the matinee.

Her mama was that beautiful. Elsie felt double bad for what she had done.

"Now come on around to the Colored waiting room and stop all this crazy business," Luther Mae huffed. She had regained her proper church-lady self. Shifting her worn old pocketbook on her arm, she grabbed Elsie's hand and marched up to the weather-beaten wood door.

Elsie couldn't help rolling her eyes up to the black letters standing out on the white metal sign nailed over the door. *COLORED ONLY*, it shouted without making any noise at all. It couldn't fade, it couldn't fall—couldn't be worn away by wind or rain. That sign would last until hell froze over, Elsie thought.

"How y'all do?" Luther Mae greeted everybody, but nobody in particular, as they walked inside.

The Colored waiting room was thick with bodies and

voices and heat so heavy that the air felt damp. A beat-up old fan chugged around and around, using its last gasps to try to make a difference. Elsie was almost hypnotized by its uselessness, staring with her mouth open as Luther Mae kept her march up to the frosted glass window.

She rapped on it sharply. Nobody came. Nobody called out "Just a minute, please" or even "Hold on, I'm coming!"

Luther Mae full-out knocked the second time. Her knuckles were hard; they were loud. The frosted glass shook, but nobody came.

Elsie looked upside her mother's head and saw the sweat in little tiny beads around her hairline; she had gotten a press and curl only yesterday. The back of Luther Mae's neck was creeping up red, and Elsie was suddenly mortified at holding up everything so that she could try her little game at the front door.

This wasn't even her own doctor's appointment. It was Luther Mae who'd been having "spells," fainting over her sewing machine at the tailor's shop where she worked. And once at the Piggly Wiggly when Elsie was pushing the cart on another aisle. Papa had tried to say she might be expecting another baby, but even Elsie knew that her Mama was not hoping for that.

"Well, where are they *at*?" Luther Mae rested her pocketbook on the window ledge, briefly touching her forehead on the glass. It seemed like she was peering in, but Elsie knew better.

"Mama, come on and sit down. I'll stand at the window for you." Elsie took her mother's elbow and looked around for a seat. The six or seven rickety folding chairs were all taken. A teenaged boy slouched against one drab wall with his arm twisted crookedly in a makeshift sling torn from a bedsheet. The woman pacing back and forth past him was rocking a baby who wheezed and coughed a deep cough. Elsie felt her mother drooping.

"I'm okay, I'm okay!" she whispered harshly.

"Here, baby. Is that Luther Mae?" Elsie looked in the direction of the whiny old voice. It was one of the deaconesses from church, one so old and wizened that she had outlived four husbands. People said the walking stick that she held against her knees had been carved by her African grandfather back in slavery time. Elsie was always kind of scared to get too close to Miz Butler, because she suspected that those milky gray eyes could look down into her soul.

Then she would know that Elsie was itching to shake things up, to *do* something . . .

"Sister Butler—" Elsie's mother tried, but couldn't quite finish her weak protest.

Miz Butler flipped up the end of her cane and nudged a man in rough work clothes who was sitting beside her. He jumped and cut his eyes at her, but she smiled and said, "Thank you, son. We all in here tryin' to get help, ain't that right?"

Elsie suppressed a giggle as the man eased up from his seat, grumbling. Her mother sat down, and Elsie looked around for a magazine or something to fan her with. There was no coffee table here, no brightly colored rectangles stacked in neat rows.

"Here, child." A woman about the same age as Luther Mae, but big with child, leaned from behind Miz Butler to give Elsie a copy of *Jet* magazine.

"I read it from cover to cover. Cool your mama off with it."

"Thank the lady, Elsie," Luther Mae murmured, holding her head with one hand.

"Mama . . ." Elsie hissed in embarrassment. She was old enough to know how to behave without being told!

"Thank you, ma'am," she said. But Miz Butler snatched the magazine, her wrinkly hand brushing against Elsie's baby-smooth one. Elsie took a step back.

"We been waitin' a long time," Miz Butler said quietly. "That baby with the croup had an appointment for two o'clock, and it's long past three . . ."

"I don't never get seen on time here. I usually drive on over to the clinic in Shreveport," somebody said.

"They in there," the boy muttered. "I seen the nurse comin' in with a sack from the Dairy Queen when my daddy dropped me off. I bet they eatin' lunch!"

Just then, Luther Mae moaned and slid out of her chair onto the pink-speckled linoleum floor.

"Mama!" Elsie dropped to her knees, patting her mother's cheek. "Mama!"

"Elsie Mary, give her some air," Miz Butler

commanded. Elsie looked up, and Miz Butler fixed those eyes on her.

Elsie knew what she had to do. She stood up and walked across the Colored waiting room. She reached out and pushed the frosted window to one side.

Before she blinked, she saw them all, frozen, like actors in a scene at the movies: The freckled, red-haired nurse, with her bloodred lips in a surprised *O*, holding her hamburger in midair with her perfect manicure; ketchup dripped down on her starched white uniform. The gray-haired, portly nurse who still wore the old-fashioned pointy cap on the back of her head, standing at a file cabinet with a sheaf of records in one hand. The doctor, with a laugh stuck in his throat, his stethoscope shining like the Brylcreem in his carefully combed hair. Both his hands were shoved into the pockets of his bright white coat. Elsie could clearly read the words *Dr. F. Baker* embroidered in royal blue script over his breast pocket. Immediately, she recognized it as her mother's work. Then she heard the clock ticking before she heard herself clearing her throat.

"Excuse me." Elsie remembered lots of things right at that moment; mostly she remembered reciting poems for Miss Caroline Washington, her third-grade teacher, the one who wore Peter Pan collars and tight straight skirts and who had studied at Spellman College out in Atlanta.

"Excuse me!" Elsie repeated in perfect *e–lo–cu–tion*, and the movie scene snapped back into action. The file drawer slammed, the hamburger's waxed paper rustled, and the doctor's shoes tapped across the floor.

"My mama has just fainted in the Colored waiting room, and could you please give her some h—er, *assistance*? Right now, please?"

The redheaded nurse, not taking her eyes off Elsie as she spread the smudge of ketchup on herself, drawled, "Well, I *never*!"

The gray-haired nurse moved with surprising quickness to push the younger one away and look out of the frosted glass window.

The doctor ignored both of them and ran out of sight. Elsie could hear him in the hall, right before he flung open the inner office door. He paused, his eyes wide, and stared at the brown crowd as if he had no idea they'd been there the whole time. As if their movie had been running on another screen all along—not a double feature, but two separate movies. This movie thing was so strong in Elsie's head that she blurted out, "The Colored waiting room is just like the balcony! You can't see us, but we can see *you*."

The doctor turned to look at Elsie in puzzlement, as if he had, in fact, just been able to see her. Then he dropped down and touched her mother's wrists, swung his stethoscope into place, and called to the nurses.

"Evelyn! It's her heart! Get me digitalis! Phoebe, call for an ambulance!"

Elsie leaned in close, hearing the word *heart*. Her

mother was pale, as pale as the redheaded nurse. Elsie smoothed back her mother's waves from her head.

"I'll never forgive myself," she heard the doctor whisper under his breath. He glanced up at Elsie just as both nurses came out, just as the *Jet* magazine lady pulled her out of the way.

Elsie looked back steadily at him, knowing that her "sweet, levelheaded" *demeanor* (as Miss Washington would have called it) did not match the blazing defiance in her eyes. But that doctor saw. And so did somebody else, Elsie realized, as something poked her shin.

"She's gone be all right, Elsie Mary. Everything gone be all right." Miz Butler croaked.

"I know," Elsie said. Her mother's eyes fluttered open as they put her on the stretcher. Elsie, full of newfound power, smiled.

# Night Searching

Mamie took a deep breath and dropped her eyes from the window to the face of Alfred's old watch. Past midnight. As she shoved her wrist back into the pocket of her apron, her arm tingled, like she had slept on it wrong. But she had not slept at all tonight. Standing in her front room in the dark, Mamie knew something had happened to her child. She wasn't a conjure woman, hadn't been born with any double veil. Yet she knew certain that somewhere in that chilly darkness, the South had tried to take him.

Knowing it made her move. She crossed over to the door and slipped into her work shoes. Opening it with the softest click, she hopped right off the edge of the porch. Steps were no use, no convenience to her. She opened the gate and took to the dirt road with her eyes wide open to the familiar shapes of the mimosa trees they had planted long ago.

At Reverend Bell's house, she looked for any signs of light or life, but they had probably gone to sleep hours ago. She was walking fast toward the street, a wide blacktopped ribbon Claiborne Tucker had sweet-talked the state into putting down for free. Tucker Lane was a winding strip between orchards of pecan trees. Behind Mamie it dead-ended smack in front of the old Tucker place. In front of her it curved for two or three miles before it met the highway leading to town.

Mamie hugged herself, hunching her muscular shoulders against the October air. She listened for the hum of the truck. It was only an old piece of truck that Alfred had gotten from some ancient White man after it quit running in a field. Alfred took it and then let it sit up on bricks in the backyard for two years. Freddie Boy had played with the thing off and on till he got it going again.

Freddie Boy could do almost anything with his hands. How often had she chastised him for messing around with scraps of wood or old machine parts? He never paid her any mind when she did. As he got older, he had figured out how to squeeze his chores in between his book learning and tinkering time.

Mamie listened hard for the sound of that smooth, rebuilt engine. The engine Freddie Boy had fixed. The truck Freddie Boy had left home driving this morning. She heard nothing.

A whisper of wind through the dry trees told her to step off the blacktop. She looked across the dry ditch to her right, squinting. If only it had been a full moon, she might be able to just see something. As it was, she had to keep blinking to make out the difference between the bushes at the bases of the trees and the nothing surrounding the bushes. She would have to go into that, and it was no longer easy or familiar.

Mamie's pecan-picking days had ended. Something like rheumatism had set in her left shoulder and dogged her so bad that Alfred had put his foot down about it, told her to turn in her sack. It was then Alfred got the electric run out to the house, and she started taking in pressing. She was good, too. Thanks to Alfred and that ironing, she had not set foot in these fields for a while, quite a while.

Even when she was a wisp of a girl, Mamie had found no beauty in greenness. She smelled no sweetness in spring grass or wide-blooming roses. It all meant work to her. Somebody, some Black body's backbreaking work spread the manure and walked the miles behind the mower and suffered the thorns.

Nature was not her friend, but she had a gut closeness to it tonight. It would have been more of a comfort to have Alfred beside her; she had to admit it at least to herself. Alfred would have placed his big hand just at her waist and held it lightly there. Just enough touch for her to feel him and all that he was without her ever being held back, or held on to.

Mamie sucked in a breath so deep that it turned into a sob.

Lord have mercy, she missed Alfred.

⁓

They had argued about Freddie Boy having the truck in the first place. Alfred ranted over how their son was too young to understand the responsibility, that he would sure enough somehow lose that truck before he got a hundred miles on it. Mamie patiently stated the facts that her husband believed but could not say. That a Colored boy like Frederick, too smart and too aware of what he didn't have and couldn't get, was not safe in the world of White men. The truck would carry him straight into such a world. Mamie knew this, and she hated it all the same.

It was Alfred who was not ready for what his son would find there. He was not ready for his boy to be challenged on his right to own anything worth something. And what if it was found out that Freddie Boy had practically made the truck himself, that he had skills and a brain to go with them? Alfred jumped angry. He'd put his fist down on the table so hard the cat leaped onto the stove, and then he roared about that.

"What is it all for, then?" Mamie raised her voice, and Freddie Boy slammed out the front door to get away from them. His part in this argument was through. "You tell me what the doggone point is for us to be sendin' him to school; us scrapin' cents together to send him down to that college, if you too scared to let him live?"

"Colored folk don't live, Mamie Lee!" Alfred spun

around to face her, and Mamie saw defeat plain in his face. This was no argument, really. They didn't disagree on the main things. His eyes were wide and bright, his long cheeks flushed. His chin trembled beneath his rough, brown beard.

Mamie had never seen him so; she knew at that moment that in twenty years she had never really seen him.

"Alfred?" She called his name quietly, wondering if the man she loved was still inside him. She had grabbed the back of a chair and held it so tight her knuckles began to ache.

"No bank's gonna give us a loan." Alfred's words dropped like rocks. Mamie felt her shoulders sag, but she jerked them up.

"Maybe—"

"Been to Baton Rouge, Lafayette, far as New Orleans, Mamie. Ain't no bank willing," he said without looking at her. "Paid our every bill on time. Got nearly a thousand dollars saved. Even the house wasn't enough, and it's paid for!"

Alfred would not look at her.

"They'll give a Colored man money to buy a new car, long as it's a Ford and last year's model. But to start a business? Damn 'em! Damn 'em to hell!" He leaned against the wall.

They had talked about starting a clothes-cleaning business ever since Freddie Boy was a baby. Mamie had built a clientele. Alfred had worked his way up from shoeshine kid to chief steward at the Tucker Hotel in his thirty years of perfect service.

It was a dream they'd had together.

"I can't give you what you want, Mamie."

"Alfred, I don't need nothin' else," she'd said.

But that blow from the banks had hurt him bad. Mamie watched him retreat deeper and deeper into himself. One gray morning a year ago, he went silently to work, and he never came home. He had left his leather-banded watch on the table beside the bed, as if time no longer meant anything to him.

Mamie had never blamed him. How could she? He had it in his head and his heart that he had failed her, and that he had raised his son to believe in a future that was a lie. And she had never realized how the weight had worn him down year after year, disappointment after disappointment, until it was too late.

Mamie breathed deep and caught the last smoky scents of fall leaves somebody had burned somewhere. She hunched her shoulders, not wanting to think about fire; not wanting to give in to the shivers running up and down her spine.

There was a rustling on the ground a few yards away, which startled her. She stopped, slowly rolling her head in the direction of the sound. Two glossy yellow eyes looked back at her. Possum. Mamie stomped her foot and watched it run. She hated those creatures. Always night searching. Always pale and bony-faced, like death.

"Frederick!" she cried out. The possum had scuttled off to the right, and so she eased the opposite way. She felt her son, her baby, so close and at the same time farther away from her than he had ever been.

She walked. For every inch her body went forward, her thoughts crept backward.

~

She had listened to the radio earlier in the day as she vigorously scrubbed Miss Virginia Walburton's cotton percale drawers on the small washboard. Miss Virginia had always been a sweet potato pie or two on the heavy side, and since she was elderly now she liked only light starch and no creases in her "intimate garments." The only hands she had ever allowed to touch her fifty pairs of lace-trimmed underwear were her own and Mamie's.

(Mamie was quite happy that Miss Virginia was so peculiar and particular. Miss Virginia had promised, if Mamie and Alfred ever opened up their own full-service place, to entrust the remainder of her extensive wardrobe to their care and attention. What did banks know about trust?)

On the radio, the man talked about dogs being set on five Colored boys who had lingered too long after their high school football game. They had run, and some of them interrupted two White waitresses walking home from work.

Mamie reached so abruptly to shut off the rest of the story that she dropped a wad of pale blue onto the floor. She'd picked it up and set it aside without rinsing it again.

She didn't need to listen to find out what happened to those boys. She knew.

Now she called out to her own. "Freddie Boy!" Her voice was hoarse, and only crickets answered. Her heart started beating fast. Thumping faster.

A short distance away, she thought she saw lightning bugs flash their behinds on and off. But it was way too late at night for them, wasn't it?

Mamie took off running toward the impossible glowing. She tripped over roots. The light grew fainter and vanished.

She stumbled and fell, hearing glass crunch under her knee just before she felt the sting of the cuts as the glass shards pushed into her skin. She glanced down as she put her hands out to steady herself.

Beer bottles. The stale stench floated up. There seemed to be a flat trail in the grass—a tire track. She located the other one by narrowing her eyes. There were bourbon jugs and more beer bottles.

Mamie fought the panic rushing between her ears. Slowly, she raised her head.

A tree stood where the swarm of lightning bugs had appeared. She was right upon it.

It was old and broad and gnarled and knotty. Mamie followed the wide trunk up to heavy branches hanging low and laden with dark ovals, nuts overlooked or never picked. The branches were surely sturdy enough for the clothesline Mamie allowed herself to view with dry eyes.

She took a step forward, and then her limbs refused to obey.

The world stopped around her.

"Freddie Boy?"

Her stomach shook, but she tried to gulp back everything. Everything.

~

It had taken them seven years to have Freddie Boy. Alfred's mother claimed she had prayed on it and accepted the fact that the Lord had been testing her by giving her son a barren woman. Mamie's own mother had brought by every herb in her experience, moved their bed around the entire house, chanted, and even studied Alfred's dreams.

Alfred never gave up. And when she was finally with child, as soon as she was sure, she told Alfred. She met him at the front door with her hair done up and wearing her best Sunday dress.

"Afternoon, Daddy," she said. He knew the happy news instantly because Mamie never referred to him by hussyfied juke-joint nicknames or in any vulgar way.

Alfred dropped to his knees and cried when Mamie told him. He wrapped his arms around her waist and laid his head where her baby was.

"Frederick Douglass Holmes, are you in there?"

Those were Alfred's first words to his son.

---

That clothesline could never hold a man. Mamie pressed her hands against her stomach as if Freddie Boy was still safe inside.

The night and Mamie's despair swallowed up the color of her son's hair and windbreaker and pants. He was a crumpled heap an arm's length away. Mamie imagined there must be blood soaking the ground. There would certainly be blood.

The line could not hold him, she told herself again.

"Frederick. Oh, my Frederick." Mamie bent over with no expectation. He was turned away from her. She hitched up her skirt and carefully stepped over him, squatting on his other side.

With a calm bordering on madness, she looked at his face.

He was seventeen. He was a beautiful seventeen-year-old boy.

His laughing chocolate eyes were swollen into two purple lumps the size of those golf balls Alfred used to bring home from his weekend job as a caddy. The flesh underneath both was even darker, and on one side seemed black with bruising. On the other his whole face jutted out horribly around his jawbone.

His face looked too big for his slender neck. Mamie thought it might wobble like the snapped neck of a turkey not-quite-killed for the Thanksgiving table. She shook her head, aware of the crazy comparison. Not quite dead.

Blood trickled from the corner of Freddie Boy's mouth. His mouth looked normal, with his wide lips parted only slightly. She could not see any of his teeth.

Freddie Boy's left sleeve was ripped away from the jacket; his hard, muscular arm was twisted back underneath his body. The angle was unnatural. His right hand was draped across his body, bloody and raked with oozing cuts. He clutched it in a fist at his groin.

Mamie sucked in a breath, but the air had gone. Her lungs burned.

He had fought. Tried to protect himself.

Both legs were bent where there were no joints. His right foot seemed to turn up, pointing to his face. What else was shattered inside him, along with his spirit?

She could not see his chest move. She could not see past the matted hair if his temples still pulsed. He did not move. She did not touch him.

It was no use wondering who had done this to him or why. She knew the beginning of Freddie Boy's story as clear as she'd known the end of the story on the radio.

Mamie held her muscles taut, and she swayed. Her eyes ached. Her womb ached. She pressed her eyes shut and recalled her baby boy's tiny new body placed warm upon hers; he had been bloody then, too. But he had screamed, and she thanked God that he was alive. Now he wasn't making a sound.

Mamie wondered if it was better that he be dead than broken up like this.

She tilted her head, and the tears streamed steady over her face like rain. All of a sudden her sorrow was so strong she could not hold herself upright against it. She slowly laid her body out on the cold, damp ground beside her son.

"Mamie Lee! I been at the house for you!"

Sounded like Alfred. Mamie raised her chin just to see across her son's still chest.

It was Alfred's lankly self, loping though the grass. There was a fire in his step, and a fire in his eyes that lit up Mamie's night.

Alfred was standing over them.

"We ain't givin' them our boy, Mamie," he said, lifting her up to rest beside him. She inhaled his man-ness.

"We ain't lettin' them take our son."

"Alfred!" Mamie touched him with her palm and looked back at Freddie.

She was his mother! It was a sin before God that she could think her son better off dead! A great pain seized her heart, and she regretted her awful notion. She pulled away from Alfred, feeling him move behind her, and gently touched her fingertips to their son's mouth.

"He's warm!"

"You stay with him. I'm gonna get help. You don't leave him, Mamie."

She slipped her arm under Freddie Boy's neck and gingerly raised his head as she lowered hers. She kissed the temples. She recalled his smiling little-boy face, the screeching voice begging her to "touch Eskimo noses" with him.

More tenderly than she ever had, Mamie rubbed her nose against her son's.

"Remember that song you used to sing?" Alfred was hovering over her, urging her.

"I don't remember no song, Alfred!" She wondered anxiously why he didn't go on, like he said he would.

"Yeah, you do now. Sing to him, Mamie. He'll hear you. You got a sweet, sweet voice. Remember that song? Sing it to your baby boy nice like you can."

That was Alfred to a T. Plying her with compliments to distract her mind. But he must be right. Alfred was right about the truck, wasn't he?

She ever so lightly placed a hand on Freddie's forehead. Yes, warm.

And then Alfred reached over her shoulder, putting his calloused hand on top of hers.

"You sing to him, Mamie," Alfred whispered.

Mamie licked her lips and found them dry; she forced

spit back down her throat to ease its tightness. Whatever song did Alfred mean? No lullaby came to her, so she opened her mouth, ready to go on whatever came out.

"Earth has no sor-row . . . that heaven can . . . not . . . cure . . ." The old hymn rolled out. But that was the ending, not the beginning. Mamie sniffed. She had to sing a beginning!

"Come . . . ye . . . disconsolate . . ."

"Mmm . . ."

"Where-er . . . you . . . lan-guish . . ."

The sound Freddie made was so faint that she was not sure she'd heard anything at all. Mamie choked in her singing, yet managed to keep humming. She strained to pick up more, wishing she could see the air going in and out of his lungs to be sure.

"Breathe, baby. Breathe for Mama. It's gonna be all right." Mamie looked off into the night, loving the breath back into her son.

Giant round yellow eyes were coming toward them. Flashing eyes, signaling to her. Maybe the White boys had come back and she would die together with her son. Mamie was not afraid.

The lights stopped. She heard voices calling out to her.

"Mamie! Mamie Lee Holmes!"

Bodies, people were walking out of the light.

"We come for you, Mamie!" She saw the grizzled white top of Reverend Bell's head. He loomed out of the light. She blinked, seeing his sons and the shimmering pink face of Doctor Waskom behind him. Mamie threw her head back and gasped for breath.

This was the doctor who'd set Freddie's broken arm when he was ten, who had handled him like he was any hurting child. The tears blinded her to the flurry of what went on around her next; she only was sure that she did not let them take Freddie away from her arms.

"W-Where's Alfred?" she hiccupped, finally allowing the doctor to put himself between her and her baby. Reverend Bell took off his coat and threw it over her hunched shoulders.

"Mamie, honey, Alfred ain't here."

Mamie looked at him for a minute, then turned back to the doctor.

"He'll live? Our boy will make it?" she asked. The doctor was grim-faced as he met her eyes.

"Can't promise, Mamie," he answered. "If he does, he won't ever be the same."

Mamie believed him. She believed that if Freddie survived, he would live hard, and hurt, never use that mind or those gifted hands the same way again.

Maybe his life wouldn't be much different from what it would have been if none of this had ever happened, she thought. His life would have been hard, and hurtful, and hardly ever right, even if this night had never happened.

"You hear me, Mamie? Child, Alfred ain't here. My wife saw you wandering in the middle of the night and sent us after you. Mamie?"

Mamie jerked away from him, quivering. Alfred had been with her. She didn't care what anybody said. How? Somehow.

Awe shook her till Reverend Bell's coat fell away, till she could hear nothing but Alfred calling to her from far off.

"Come and get him, Alfred!" she murmured, so nobody else could hear. "Come on and take Freddie with you. Come on, come on."

Mamie arched her head over her shoulder, listening for Alfred to answer.

"Give me that syringe! Hurry!" She heard the doctor instead. The doctor was frantic. She heard him pumping Freddie's chest, and she heard the pumping stop.

Reverend Bell wailed, "Oh, Lord have mercy on his soul!"

Mamie bowed her head.

She looked up at the sky and saw no stars. No moon.

# Colorstruck

"She is black, but comely, O ye daughters of Jerusalem!"

Hazel dropped the stack of envelopes she'd just pulled from the mailbox. She clucked at her own clumsiness and bent to pick them up, rising just in time to spy the source of that rich baritone voice. Next door, over the honeysuckle-draped wire fence, an intense pair of dark eyes was fixed on her.

"If Reverend Clark catches you flirting with scripture, JC—" She couldn't decide how to finish the reprimand, partially because it wasn't all that genuine. She resented his comment about being black, despite the fact that out of all six Reed sisters, she was sure enough the darkest in the bunch. But then, she took great satisfaction in his noticing her . . . *comeliness.*

"Girl, Reverend Clark got hot blood runnin' through his veins too. How come you think he can burn up the pulpit like he does every Sunday? And speaking of Sunday, what you doin' next Saturday night?"

Hazel burst into tinkling laughter and slapped the mail against her thigh as she strode back up the sloping yard to Miss Clotille's porch. She never answered him. One thing she had learned well from Miss Clotille, her employer since she'd turned thirteen six years ago, was how to be coy. At the steps, she flung a broad smile over her shoulder.

JC continued to eyeball the scenery, propping his elbow up on the handle of the lawnmower he'd pushed from Miss Clotille's over to his next job.

"You as fine as plum wine, Hazel Mozella Reed! You hear me?" he shouted at the slamming screen door.

Hazel stopped at the mirror hanging over the marble hall table and took a long drink of herself. She prayed thanks every night for the natural waves—Indian hair, her grandmother Mama Vee called it—that fell back from her temples, even when she sweated her head. She had long ago learned to painstakingly arch her heavy eyebrows and believed they were now a "perfect accent to her high cheekbones and full, yet never broad lips."

Hazel couldn't help but think of the words Madame Florence Ethel Ameal-Jones had used to describe the "Ideal Colored Woman" in the last issue of Miss Clotille's *Half-Century Magazine*. Yes, Hazel thought, I have all of those attributes except one, and I'm working on that! She leaned in closer to her reflection and tilted her head to look.

There *was* a difference! Clear as day, she could see that

there was. She raised trembling fingers to touch her cheek.

"Haaazelll? Is that postman late again?"

Miss Clotille was the only person Hazel had ever heard say "postman" instead of "mailman," "etiquette" instead of "manners," and "despise" instead of "hate." Miss Clotille often described herself as "unique," and Hazel agreed. "One-of-a-kind crazy," Hazel's sister Jurdine called Miss Clotille. But Jurdine was just jealous that she wasn't getting culture and wisdom on her job plucking chickens out at Garrett's Farm.

"No, ma'am, he was on time. I'm coming!"

Hazel didn't rush, but she moved quickly. Her bare feet made no sound on the gleaming wood floor that she had polished yesterday. Miss Clotille kept telling her that it was unseemly for a young woman to go around without shoes in public, but Hazel differed with her on that point: she felt it was unseemly for a housekeeper to scuff her own floors on purpose.

At the door of Miss Clotille's bedroom Hazel paused to organize the various magazines and bills and invitations by size, and then she waited.

"Oh! There you are." The faint dust of rouge rose up from the dressing table as Miss Clotille replaced her powder puff and turned to Hazel expectantly.

They always had their little ceremonies. Hazel supposed these were Miss Clotille's attempts—having no husband, no children, and no sisters or brothers—to mimic a regular family's routines. And though there were so many things about Miss Clotille that Hazel not only admired but worked with great concentration to emulate, Hazel firmly believed she would hear a *Mrs.* and a *Mama* in her own near future.

Hazel handed over the mail and smiled.

"Thank you, dear," Miss Clotille said sweetly. "And would you call for Mr. Tom to bring the car for me at twelve thirty?"

Hazel crossed the room to open the huge mahogany chifferobe.

"Yes, ma'am. Now, I don't directly recall . . . you wearing the green or the purple to your luncheon?"

"Oh, Hazel! *Are* you wearing! *Are* you! And they're *teal* and *magenta*, my dear. I'll be wearing the magenta. It matches my lipstick."

Hazel smiled again and took out the mentioned dress. She didn't mind being corrected. Working for somebody like Miss Clotille might be the best education she would ever get, since the chances were slim to none that her family could send her to college.

"I think the magenta is perfect, Miss Clotille."

Mama Vee always claimed Clotille Henderson had been a woman when she was a girl, but Miss Clotille was well-preserved and determined, even if she was nearly sixty. She was tiny—the tips of her pink silk mules barely touched the floor when she sat at her dressing table. But what Miss Clotille lacked in stature had never held her back in any of the classrooms where she'd taught countless corn-fed country girls and rough, cotton-picking boys. Hazel fervently believed that Miss Clotille prevailed because she had the power of that flawless almond skin.

Her light skin commanded the right kind of attention. It spoke of her easy membership in societies and organizations and committees that would never dare ask her to suffer their paper-bag entrance tests. Her pale, sometimes pink, but never tan cheeks practically shouted down the word *Colored* on her birth certificate. The way Miss Clotille held her pointy chin high, peering boldly at everyone and anyone her path crossed, told the world that she was a female force. Everything about her combined to make Miss Clotille ideal in Hazel's estimation.

"Since I'll be gone for the afternoon, Hazel, you may leave early. That is, I'm assuming that you have everything in order." Miss Clotille raised her pencil-thin brows, but her expression was amused.

Hazel never left anything out of order. Mama Vee had worked as a maid and housekeeper for White people—people far richer than Miss Clotille could ever be—for forty-five years. Violet Jenkins's standards in "her" houses where she worked for pay were the same as they were in the tight but impeccably clean little bungalow where she and Hazel's mother, father, and sisters lived. Miss Clotille didn't know or understand that Mama Vee had already been to her house to test Hazel's cleaning ability. Hazel had passed muster for her grandmother a full year ago.

"You'll be assuming correct," she grinned.

"*Correctly*. Yes, I really thought so."

"*Correctly*," Hazel repeated, and then paused. "Miss Clotille . . . You think it would seem proper if I was to step out with JC?"

Hazel had tried to ask the question without the edge of hesitation in her voice, but failed. She sucked in her bottom lip and blinked in Miss Clotille's direction, knowing that Miss Clotille was fully aware of her own power.

"If you *were* to step out?"

"Yes, ma'am."

"Is that Johnson Johnson you're speaking of?" Miss Clotille asked. "The boy who cuts my grass?"

"Yes, ma'am!" Hazel answered quickly. "But JC only does that part-time. He's a full-time janitor over at the Normal College, and he's a fine piano player!"

Miss Clotille blinked just once. "Not in a juke joint, I hope!"

Hazel shook her head vigorously. "Oh, no! He plays both services over at Galilee Baptist Church. His mama is choir director!" Hazel thought, then added, "He is a very upstanding gentleman."

"Well, then, if you know that, dear, you certainly don't need any permission from me. What do your parents think of him?"

Hazel didn't exactly want to say that, though her mother was lukewarm over it, her father was pleased as punch over possibly having one of his girls walk down the aisle—even though Hazel had never done as much as sing a solo to JC's accompaniment at nine o'clock service.

"They don't have no complaints," she said honestly.

"*Any* complaints. Good. He has asked you out, I suppose? Where to?"

"Er . . . to the movies next weekend," Hazel lied. The dance was at the juke joint.

"You have a good time."

Hazel smiled as she hooked the back of Miss Clotille's magenta chiffon. She floated out of the room, lifted by expectation and filled with imaginative plans.

"Girl, what in the devil are you still *doing* in there? I gotta work a night shift!" Jurdine's whine was more shrill than usual. She hated the night shift, she said, because by then the chickens' stink had turned into a vapor that seeped into her hair and skin.

Hazel was thankful to God that she didn't have that job, though it allowed her sister to own two pairs of fancy dress shoes and get her hats custom made.

"Hazel Mozella, if you don't come out of there, I'm gonna call Daddy!"

Hazel smirked at her reflection in the bathroom mirror and continued to rub the skin cream slathered onto her face in slow, circular movements. The instructions said to coat the skin evenly for best effects. And so far, the product had worked beautifully; she wasn't going to mess it up now!

"MAAAMMMAAA!" Jurdine was banging harder.

Hazel ran the cold water and splashed it up, reaching for a clean facecloth. Her fingers tingled as they grabbed the dry square. Mama Vee must have used too much bleach again, she thought, patting her cheeks dry.

There was a swift clicking of heels on the linoleum outside the door, and Hazel hurried to push the glass jar back inside its box and shove the box into a brown paper bag. She checked herself in the mirror and turned on the faucet to rinse the sink.

"Gal, you hold your sister up from making money and I'ma take it out of your black behind!" Mama Vee barked, and Hazel's bones rattled along with the window. She tossed the bag into the half-full laundry hamper and quickly fluffed up her father's dirty work pants on top. Taking a deep breath, she flushed the toilet and opened the door.

Jurdine huffed and pushed past. Hazel noticed curiously that she was wearing perfume. She didn't bother to comment, though. Mama Vee's stern gray-green eyes were burning in her yellow face.

"Why you stay up in that mirror, I do not know," she said, narrowing those eyes at Hazel. "Lookin' won't make you no lighter!"

Long ago, Hazel had taught herself not to wince. She smiled and said "No ma'am" so sweetly that Mama Vee's breath seemed suddenly sucked away, and the wide-hipped queen of the house stood angrily rooted to her spot as Hazel sashayed away.

Hazel knew that save for her dark skin, she was the spitting image of Mama Vee. Did her father's mother resent her as some kind of bitter reflection?

Hazel was turning that surprising idea over in her mind when she entered the kitchen and slipped into her chair. Her mother gave her a quick, harried nod from the stove, and sisters buzzed everywhere, distracting her from her grandmother's whys and wherefores.

Velma Jean was their mother's shadow, stirring with the same long nut-brown hands; easing out and around their mother as they placed serving dishes on the table in a perfect rhythm. It was their supper dance.

Violet, whose attitudes were in every way the same as her namesake's, shook her mane of thick brown curls, sucked her teeth impatiently, and began instantly to rearrange the plates her twin had only just set down. They used to be identical, but no one understood how Violet had become so skinny and sour over barely seventeen years.

Miriam had already scrunched her small self into her chair at the far end of the crowded table. She smiled her round, suntanned face up at Hazel from some library book that she was deep into reading. And from the back porch, everyone could hear Baby George slamming and stomping off her basketball and boy scents before she came in and boldly denied both.

My happy family, Hazel thought. Someday I will have

my own and love it as much as this one. Me and Johnson Caesar Johnson. Mrs. Hazel Mozella Reed-Johnson . . .

"Hey, Brown Sugar!" Daddy shared his gap-toothed grin with her, and she felt her shoulders relax.

"Hey, Daddy." Hazel raised herself to give him a peck on the cheek. He looked tired, the way any man who worked three jobs to support all his women would. As Hazel sat back down, she wondered for a fleeting moment if JC would look tired too, one day. He already had as many jobs as her daddy did, and she wanted a magazine-perfect house and two or three children with it!

"Guess what?" Baby George came breathless beside Hazel, swinging her chair around backward to perch on it. Her face was glowing golden with a pink hint of excitement, and the fat black braids she had wound up tight around her head looked like the crown of some wild, happy queen—or king.

"We beat the pants off them Garret Farm boys, fifty-five to thirty-two!"

"I hope you don't really mean that!" Hazel laughed and poured her father a full glass of sweet tea. She still wasn't sure if her sister—who wasn't actually the baby—carried on this sports craziness because she wanted to be around the boys, or because she wanted to *be* a boy. As Velma Jean often whispered, the jury was still out on that.

"Lord, girl! Set that chair straight!" Mama Vee had made her way into the room. She shook her head and turned to set the big platter of chicken in front of Daddy.

"Good thing Jurdine has to work tonight!" Miriam said, eyeing the chicken cheerfully and sliding her closed book onto her lap.

"If it wasn't for Jurdine, we wouldn't be having no chicken," Violet murmured. Hazel couldn't tell if her sister thought that was a good or bad thing, but she didn't ask her to clarify. Nobody wanted Violet to get started. "Pontificating" was what Miss Clotille called it.

Daddy motioned to Baby George without speaking, and she sheepishly rearranged her chair and herself, giving him a one-sided grin that was gapped like his. Whether their mother had known it or not, she had certainly marked what she'd thought was her last baby and hoped-for son. When another girl had popped out into Daddy's hands on the kitchen floor, Mama called her George anyway. And Daddy, proud as ever, was the one who'd decided they better soften it with "Ann." The "Baby" part had stuck, even after Miriam had surprised them all ten years ago. Any way it worked out, George was her father's child more than any of the others.

And once again, when Hazel looked under her eyes at them while Daddy said a long grace, she wondered for the hundredth time how the blood had mixed up to make *her* so different from everybody else. Well, look so different. It shouldn't matter in a family, and mostly it didn't. But to Mama Vee, Hazel was the stain she couldn't clean away.

"Amen," their voices united to end the prayer. Glasses and plates and forks clinked.

"Oh! Hazel!" Baby George speared a tomato and looked at her sister with bright gray-green eyes. "Lucky Johnson asked me to the dance next Saturday. Didn't JC ask you?"

Everything clattered to a stop, and Hazel found herself almost choking. First of all, a boy had asked Baby George to a dance, *and she was happy about it*? And secondly, JC had discussed his plans with his brother, and now her sister—her whole family—knew?

Mama's head whipped from one side to the other, and all she could get out was sputter.

"Unbelievable!" Velma Jean and Violet were so surprised that their twin-speak flared up and they said the exact same word at the exact same time.

"I declare, these girls are so fast! Evelyn, you need to do something about your fast girls," Mama Vee muttered with a frown at her rice and gravy.

Only Daddy didn't seem to need to recover from anything.

"Why, ain't this nice?" He nodded slowly at Hazel first, then Baby George in turn. "They call that a double date, and how 'bout it's two brothers and two sisters? Brown Sugar and Baby George is growin' up into women!"

Mama coughed. "Now, George, I don't know about all that. Hazel, maybe . . . but George Ann's only fifteen!"

Baby George opened her mouth to protest, turning beet red, but no words came out and she looked helplessly at Hazel. She really wanted this! Hazel was shocked at George's moment of weakness, but she wasn't going to let her down. "It's all right, Mama. Lucky and JC are real respectable boys. And you always say George Ann ought to be involved in more ladylike activities. Besides, I'll be right there. I'll be her *chaperone*."

In some strange way, Miss Clotille had come to the Reed dinner table. Hazel ran a glance past her grandmother's slow boil, over the twins' open-mouthed stares, and Miriam's giggles to look at her parents.

"Well!" Mama breathed. Something like a twinkle sparkled behind the rims of her black eyeglasses. "I guess Miss Clotille has sunk a whole lot of the fine points of culture into you after all, Hazel. I—I don't know what I'll make of you if she gets you off to some college . . ." her words trailed off, almost wistfully.

Hazel had once spoken to Miss Clotille about the possibility of training at the Colored Normal College, maybe following her footsteps to a classroom somewhere, but Miss Clotille had declined to give advice, saying she didn't want her to have false hopes. Now Hazel's hopes weren't certain, and she wasn't sure where any college money would come from. Still, a little bit of her had wished for a different kind of reaction.

So she said nothing to Mama.

"That's fine. Just fine," Daddy said, looking at Hazel hard. "You a girl with natural smarts, Sugar. If life takes you along the school way, that's all right. And if you have an honest working life, that's all right too. You got good sense, and that's what counts. George Ann couldn't have a better one to look up to." He said that last sentence with finality and then proceeded to sprinkle hot sauce onto his field peas before he stirred them into the mound of rice covering his plate.

Hazel swallowed. "Thank you, Daddy." She reached for Baby George's hand under the table and squeezed it; her sister squeezed back.

"Girl, I'm the luckiest man on God's green Earth!" JC grabbed both of Hazel's hands and swung her around as if they were already on the dance floor. Hazel felt warm inside and flushed outside. She didn't resist when JC looped one of his long arms inside hers.

"I gotta get to the grocery and back before Miss Clotille comes home!" she protested feebly.

"Let me walk you piece of the way," he crooned into her ear.

Hazel slowed down enough to let him fall in step with her. On Tuesdays Miss Clotille had her teacher's meeting and some committee meetings, so Hazel had plenty of time to pick up the few items for her refrigerator.

For now, she could pay attention to how solid JC's shoulder was against hers, and how pleasantly manly he smelled, even though he'd been clipping hedges when he saw her. They strolled. Hazel wished she could be seen, but this was a working neighborhood and it was only three o'clock. Even the old people were still inside listening to their radio programs or dozing at this time of day.

"Hazel, I gotta tell you something."

"What is it?" Hazel didn't know him as well as she planned to, but she heard the romance creep out of his voice. She looked up sharply.

There wasn't a trace of dishonesty in his face. He stopped and swallowed. Hazel watched his Adam's apple slide up and down. He tightened his grip on her hand the same way she'd done to Baby George, and that was comforting.

"I took on another job."

"That's all? I have to tell you, JC, that I do like a hardworking man." She squinted up at him. His chiseled cheekbones glistened in the afternoon sun. "I'm glad. But what I mean to tell you is that—well, I know you're a real upright kinda girl—and—"

"You haven't broken the law, have you?"

"No! No! I joined a band, Hazel. A jazz band."

Hazel sighed and smiled. "Well, honey, I know you're a musician! That seems natural to me."

He grinned. His teeth were the straightest, whitest teeth Hazel had ever seen on a man. She figured they had never seen tobacco, those pretty teeth. But it was clear that JC wasn't through talking. Hazel waited patiently, and she could tell that he appreciated her calmness.

"I'm glad. The thing is, I worked last weekend. We did this gig, you know—that's what we call a performance—and it was at a private club."

Hazel knew what that meant. It meant a restricted club. A White club. Why would she take exception to that? The money was still green, wasn't it? She kept listening. JC cocked his head to one side, almost like he wanted to see her better.

"This was last Saturday night," he said carefully. Hazel nodded.

"These White men were having a party. They had some gambling and they were all liquored up and we played till two in the morning. The thing is, we weren't the only . . . uh . . . entertainment. Hazel, there was women there, women they hired to come. Jurdine was one of the women." He took a breath. "I saw her leave with one of 'em."

Hazel's knees went numb, and she felt herself drifting from the great height of truth down to the hard reality of lies. Last Saturday night. When Jurdine had worn perfume to the night shift.

"Hey, baby! Are you okay? I knew I shouldn't have said anything . . . Hazel, I'm sorry!" She was in his arms, but it wasn't the way she'd dreamed it would be. Her heart was racing, and she could barely speak.

"Hazel! Doggone it, I shoulda kept my big mouth—"

"It's all right . . . " she forced the words out, though her stomach was fluttering and she was about to throw up. JC held onto her. She fought to get control over her body and her mind, which had seemed to go blank. ". . . Just . . . just don't tell nobody else. No one else, please?" She was weak, but she struggled to get to her feet. JC lifted her.

"Whatever you say, Hazel. I only thought that somebody in the family should know, in case . . ." he faltered. Hazel turned to look at him.

"In case what?" she asked, still unable to put all the information together and accept the real facts he had presented.

"In case something happens to her." JC had lowered his voice, and Hazel was suddenly alert. Jurdine was living dangerously. "I don't think you're in the shape to go to the grocery by yourself," he said. "Let me walk you over there and back. Maybe you ought to go home."

Hazel shook her head vigorously, and the twist of hair at her neck fell. Waves cascaded against her skin, making her feel feverish. She couldn't go home. There would be questions, nosy questions. And she couldn't leave Miss Clotille's without putting things in order—there would be questions in that quarter, too.

"No, I can make it if you help me. When I get back to Miss Clotille's I can sit a while and get myself together. I have to figure out what to do with what you told me . . . I know you did what you thought was best, JC." She managed to smile.

He lightly touched her hair. "Excuse me, Hazel Mozella Reed, but you are awfully beautiful with your hair down."

An orange school bus swung around the nearest corner and surrounded them with screeches and screams. Hazel straightened her back and started to walk.

"You're excused, Johnson Caesar Johnson," she said, reaching for his hand.

When Hazel stepped back into her house later that afternoon, she remembered that on Tuesdays, Mama and Daddy went straight from work to their deacon and deaconess board meetings at the church. So she took a deep breath of relief as she crossed the threshold. Laughter and girls' gossip floated from the kitchen to meet her, and the air was heavy with the smell of sizzling Royal Crown Hair Dressing. Hazel untied her shoes near the door and carried them toward the back of the house.

"Ouch! You singed me!" Baby George's complaint was muffled by the fact that her chin was pushed down against her chest. Velma Jean sat on a high stool over her sister; one hand grasped a shock of tightly curled hair, the other was raised and holding the smoking hot comb. Miriam sat at the table, flipping the pages of one of Hazel's borrowed *Half-Century* magazines.

Hazel shook her head and laughed, for a moment forgetting the awful news that she was holding. "What are y'all doing in here, messing up Mama's kitchen?" She pulled out a chair and dropped into it.

"Trying to make a woman out of this sister thing we got." Violet appeared with an armful of dresses, sucking her teeth. "George, have you *ever* worn a decent dress?"

George mumbled and scrunched even further down into the chair.

"I'ma hit you in the head if you don't sit still!" Velma Jean warned.

"Hazel, how come you got the words in this advertisement underlined with an ink pen?" Miriam was bending close over a page in the back of the magazine. Hazel swiftly snatched it away, but Violet's keen eyes had already seen.

"You using *bleaching cream*?" Violet shrieked.

The hot comb clinked onto the burner, and Velma Jean actually jerked George Ann's head up. All eyes were on Hazel.

Suddenly she felt accused and defensive. Her throat went dry.

"Oh no, Hazel." Velma Jean's eyes teared.

"That's just crazy!" Baby George shook her head, and the smooth, already pressed waves moved like a black curtain.

"Don't tell me you takin' Mama Vee and Jurdine seriously!" Violet exploded, dropping her frown to the magazine. "Everybody knows how colorstruck they are!"

"Mama says a woman who tries to change her natural beauty is a fool! But you're smart, Hazel!" Miriam said. "You could be a teacher, you could be just like Miss Clotille."

Miriam's little-girl remarks hit just too close to the truth. Hazel clutched the magazine in her sweating hands.

She wanted to leave the room, but her legs were weak again. Yes, their mother said that. Mama worked hard and mothered hard and prayed hard, and still had her looks and her devoted husband. Miss Clotille had money and creamy skin and respect. Hazel coveted all that. But what were her chances? She was milk chocolate in a world where that was the same as mud.

"It—it's just a beauty treatment. That's all it is."

"Beauty, my ass." Violet hissed.

"Hazel, you're already beautiful!" said Miriam.

Hazel gave her a shaky smile in return.

"Could we get off Hazel and get back to beautifying *me*?" George Ann pleaded, wagging her half-straight, half-braided head. Violet held up the two dresses she'd been wrinkling in her arms. Both were Jurdine's. Both were expensive.

Hazel shook her head, guessing how her sister had paid for them. Baby George's first social occasion couldn't be tainted with that.

"Don't nobody want to hear Jurdine ranting over those scraps of material. I have a nice seersucker, George, that I only wore one time. I know it would fit you. Let me pull it out." Hazel dragged herself up from the table.

"Thanks, Hazey!" George Ann said.

Violet followed Hazel into the hallway toward their bedroom. She gripped Hazel's elbow once they were out of earshot of the kitchen.

"I saw that advertisement. You'd better stop messing with that shit. It'll kill you."

Hazel gently pulled her arm away. "When did you get such a nasty mouth?"

On Thursday evening, Hazel locked herself in the bathroom after dinner. She sat on the closed toilet and turned the glass jar in her hands, reading the label aloud softly. "*Beauty Queen Complexion Clarifier . . . Guaranteed to brighten, lighten, and heighten your natural beauty*!" What was so wrong with that? She wondered. "*Manufactured by the Emerson Beauty Company, Emerson, Georgia.*" But nowhere inside the pretty scrollwork border did the label tell what, exactly, this miracle-working product was manufactured *with*. Her mind wandered back to her sisters' reactions. Everybody called it bleaching cream . . . but did it really have bleach in it?

She blinked at the jugs and containers of cleaning products lined neatly under the sink. Too much bleach could eat through linens and clothes. Surely they couldn't have put something like that into a skin cream, could they?

She thought of the smelly but fascinating experiments she had done in chemistry class. She could ask Mr. Goodman, the teacher. She had once confided in him about her self-invented cleaning formula, and he had gotten all excited, talking about how she had a head for science! She had laughed at the notion, knowing that her lab grades had always been only fair to middling.

She had never read as many books as Miriam did. She read all sorts of magazines though, including that *National Geographic* when she could get her hands on it. She loved the feeling it gave her of traveling all over the world. And Daddy brought home his boss's stack of newspapers at the end of every week. Hazel pored over them. It never mattered to her that the news was several days late.

She was sometimes bothered that she didn't always speak the way educated people did; none of the Reeds did. In fact, it was Miss Clotille who'd pointed that out.

Miss Clotille had always been helpful in pointing out those small things that separated the Reeds from the most cultivated, *ideal* Colored class. At every turn she had a little idea, or suggestion or correction. Miss Clotille had taken Hazel under her wing, brought her to work in her home to . . .

To what?

It occurred to her that as long as Hazel felt too brown and far from correct, Miss Clotille's tiny person stayed lofty, light, and proud.

Sudden, urgent tapping on the door interrupted Hazel's discoveries.

"Hazel! I need to get in there!" Without thinking, Hazel leaned to open the door.

Jurdine rushed to the mirror. In silence, Hazel watched

her older sister, conscious for the first time of how much Jurdine and Miss Clotille were alike.

Jurdine wasn't small, but she was perfect in figure, curving exactly where she should. She had lovely ankles. Her creamy skin had to be some kind of throwback to Mama Vee's White grandfather, and the blood mix had straightened every curl out of Jurdine's shoulder-length black hair even when it was wet. She had the full lips and wide dark eyes of their father, and the only thing of Mama's that Jurdine had gotten was the husky tone of her words.

The ideal Colored woman.

Jurdine must have felt her sister's stare, because she paused and narrowed her eyes. She spun around, smoothing the lines of her tight black skirt. The white explosion of ruffles she wore to top it fell away neatly from her ample cleavage, which she shook in Hazel's stunned direction.

"What?" she breathed arrogantly.

"Where are you going this time of night?"

"Not to any dance with a piss-poor piano player!" Jurdine smacked her ruby lips together to even her lipstick. She had just the right hint of rouge on her cheeks.

Hazel set her jaw. She didn't want to be provoked, and it was so easy for Jurdine, who had learned from the mistress of provocation in this house, their grandmother.

"Does he know you're secretly trying to make yourself light, bright, and damned near White—like me?"

Hazel tried to grip the jar tightly, but it slipped from her fingers and rolled to the floor. Jurdine bent to pick it up.

"You are what you are, Hazey," she said, throwing the words out as if Hazel's being anything wasn't important in the scheme of life.

"And what are you, Jurdine Marie? Johnson C. Johnson gets paid to play the piano. What you get paid to do, Jurdine?"

Jurdine blanched.

"How many chickens are you gonna pluck tonight when you sneak out?"

The pride slumped out of her shoulders. Her luscious lips parted and closed, but she couldn't seem to manage even a quick drop of meanness.

Hazel stood up, lightheaded—so much had changed, so much was changing—and opened the bathroom door. "You better be careful, Jurdine." Hazel pulled the door closed behind her with a soft click and made her way to the bedroom, where she collapsed across the bed she would share with Jurdine whenever she came home. If she came home.

Hazel didn't sleep. Later, in the last humid hours of night, she felt Jurdine's presence in the room, felt the mattress move as she sat to peel off her clothes and push them carelessly underneath the bed. Hazel heard the soft crying and knew she wasn't meant to. She almost got up to give comfort.

But she didn't. She curled away from the pain to dream.

The next morning Hazel felt terrible when she woke. While she'd dreamed, a sadness about Jurdine and Miss Clotille had somehow settled in her bones. Even thinking of getting up seemed too much effort. She blinked in surprise at the empty, quiet room.

Jurdine was long gone, and so were Velma Jean and Violet. Miriam and George Ann's cots were already closed and rolled into the corner. Hazel pushed herself up onto an elbow. What time was it?

"Chile, lay back in that bed!" Mama Vee bustled in with a tin mug of what smelled like peppermint tea. Hazel obeyed, because her head and stomach had jiggled in time with each other when she moved. She lay back on the pillow as her grandmother came around.

"Jurdine said you tossed and turned all night, and Evelyn came in here and said she felt a fever on you. I don't have time to do no coddling, just here's this tea to settle your stomach."

Mama Vee was wearing her starched black uniform, and her smooth silver hair was sleek under a hairnet. She put the cup on the small bedside table and stood over Hazel like a doctor who could examine with x-ray eyes.

"'Course, I don't believe it's your stomach that needs settling—I believe it's your hard, kinky head!"

Hazel closed her eyes. It was no use trying to point out to Mama Vee that her hair had never been crinkly or kinky; just as it would never be any use trying to convince her the truth was that being *any* shade of brown was simply being Black to the folks Mama Vee wanted to impress. Hazel rolled away from her grandmother, pulling her knees up to meet her chin as she lay on her side. Her joints ached.

"You surly wench! I'll send word round to the school and Miss Clotille that you won't be comin' to work today." Mama Vee's voice receded as she marched away. "Seems to me, somebody in your position would take her job more serious . . ."

Hazel wanted to holler that Jurdine took her job real serious, but she didn't have it in her. Jurdine was only trying in her own way to do the same thing as Hazel. She wanted more out of her life than an ordinary Colored one—or Negro or Black one—was likely to provide.

When Mama Vee was long gone, Hazel slept fitfully. Thoughts skittered in her semiconscious mind between stretches of nothing.

"Hazel! Hazel!" Was that Jurdine? Couldn't be . . . Hazel slowly forced her heavy eyelids open. The light filtering underneath the half-pulled shade was different. She was overwhelmed by the scent of chicken feathers and sweet perfume. Her stomach turned and cramped. Yes, Jurdine.

Hazel blinked up at the pale face.

"W-What?"

"I brought you a surprise. Wake up!" Jurdine was grinning. Hazel took a deep breath. She still felt something awful.

"Come on, girl. Sit up, now. Let me smooth your hair. And this gown . . ." Jurdine looked around quickly and grabbed a blouse from the twins' bed. She threw it over Hazel's shoulders and arranged it like a bed jacket.

"What in the world are you doing?" Hazel asked, wanting to resist her sister's out-of-character fussing and concern.

"There!" Jurdine stood back for a moment. "Now, close your eyes."

Hazel sucked her teeth in irritation. "For real, Hazel! It's a big surprise, but I have to give it to you in a hurry, before anybody gets home!"

Hazel frowned and obeyed.

"Don't make that ugly face!" Jurdine said. "You'll be sorry!"

"Jurdine—"

"Okay, open your eyes. Surprise!"

Hazel turned in the direction of her sister's voice, and there in the bedroom doorway stood Johnson C. Johnson. He had on his crisp khaki uniform, but he had topped it with a cocky straw Panama. He swept off his hat with one hand; with the other he held out a bunch of roses from Reverend Clark's yard. Hazel's physical and mental agitation eased, and she managed to smile.

"Excuse me for imposing, Hazel Mozella Reed. But your sister here found me and said you were laid up, and I knew it must be serious because I never heard of you missing school or work or anything. And I thought . . . maybe you might not be up for tomorrow night, so—"

Hazel wanted to say "No!" but a wave of nausea shook her. As she watched JC's expression change from simple caring to worry, someone else banged into the house and Jurdine's voice was soon in argument with Baby George's.

"How come I can't . . ." George almost knocked JC down shouldering her way into the bedroom. "Oh. Hey, JC," she said, plopping onto the bed.

"Hazel! I just happened to mention to Mr. Goodman about the bleaching cream, and—"

"What?" Hazel moaned.

"George Ann, one day your mouth is gonna write a check your ass can't cover!" Jurdine fumed.

"Bleaching cream?" JC walked around the bed and sat so close that Hazel could look straight into his questioning eyes. There was no blame there, only love. Love! She couldn't speak.

George, however, had words bursting out. "Yes! And no wonder you're down. Do you know what Mr. Goodman said is in that mess? Mercury! Mercury, Hazel!"

Hazel couldn't answer. A pain seized her and she jerked her knees up, dry heaving. She felt George take her hand, and she heard Jurdine screaming in the background. But closest to her ear was JC's strong authority.

"Hazel, we're takin' you to the hospital."

She passed clean out.

"Oh, Hazel, you look so peaked." Hazel found it strange that Daddy didn't use his regular nickname for her. If she was dreaming again . . .

She was not. She woke up feeling very weak, and her father was really standing over her. She wasn't at home anymore. The smell of medicines and cleaning products made her nose tingle. There was a bright white curtain curving around the narrow bed.

"I'm in the hospital, Daddy?" she asked. Her voice sounded small and far away.

"Yes, baby, yes," Mama answered.

Hazel turned her head on the pillow. Her mother's face was strained. And scared. Hazel tried to reach out to her and realized that the bottom half of her body was numb. Her eyes widened.

"What happened?" was all she could get out. Was she paralyzed? How? What?

The metal rings holding the curtain suddenly slid back noisily. A white-coated, white-haired White man frowned at Hazel. When he moved, she saw a black-haired ghost cowering behind him, trembling in an ugly work smock. Jurdine.

Hazel blinked and licked her dry lips, attempting to put her confusion into words.

"Don't try to talk just yet." The doctor unclipped a chart from the bed and read it over quickly, then shoved it under his arm.

Hazel had a flashed memory of JC's muscular arms, and a straw hat, and big old pink roses . . .

"George? Evelyn? I'm Dr. Barton."

Barton, Hazel thought. Like Clara Barton, the nurse.

Was he kin to her? Hazel wanted to rid her head of these random notions . . . She wrinkled her forehead and attempted to focus.

"And you, child, must be the naughty one."

Hazel felt offended, and that familiar emotion cleared her wits. "How come I can't move?" she challenged. The doctor looked directly at her.

"Because, Hazel, you are still under anesthesia. You had a kidney removed."

Hazel shivered as her parents gasped.

"Oh, you'll recover all right. There are plenty folks who live normal lives with one kidney. Some are born with only one. But you—you poisoned yours, with mercury. Your entire nervous system almost shut down. You were dying."

Hazel was shocked. She'd been bettering herself and killing herself at the same time? The devil. The devil had been doing a fine dance inside that little jar, hadn't he! And inside her head, too.

The doctor raised his eyebrows. "How long were you using that . . ."

Mama fumbled in her bag and pulled something out. "Beauty Queen Complexion Clarifier," she read in a strange, singsong voice.

The doctor took the jar and looked at it carefully. "Unhealthy, unproven, dangerous, and deadly," he finally said. "You're a handsome Colored girl. I hope you've learned your lesson."

"Yes sir," Hazel murmured, looking down at her smooth, evenly brown hands. Brown. Not any lighter. Not wrong. Just brown.

"Mother and father, I need to speak with you about your daughter's recuperation." Daddy gave Hazel a smile, Mama planted a kiss, and they followed the doctor away. Jurdine stayed at the foot of the bed.

"Oh, Hazel, what a stupid thing to do!" she said in a low voice.

"You oughta know, Jurdine."

Hazel waited for her sister's comeback, hoping that she was numbed enough to take whatever blow was coming. Instead, Jurdine blushed deeply, and Hazel could see tears welling up in her eyes.

"Hazey, I didn't mean—"

"Yeah, you always *mean*, Jurdine." Hazel cut her off and looked away. What was she apologizing for, anyway? A lifetime?

There was quiet between them. Then, as Hazel looked at Jurdine again, she didn't only seem genuinely mournful, she seemed . . . old.

Hazel was awake enough to see how ridiculous it was: Jurdine was banking on Time, and Time didn't cut deals with nobody. Even Miss Clotille's gentlemen callers had gotten scarce when the lines started creeping around her eyes and throat.

"It won't last," Hazel murmured to her sister.

"You're talkin' out of your head," Jurdine said. "And

you might as well know, being light-skinned won't get you nothin', 'cause we still poor and Colored in this lil' bitty Louisiana town . . ." She paused, biting her lip. Her tone was bitter as lemons.

"I'm not stayin', Hazel," she went on, her words running together fast. "I'm just another mouth to feed, and what I make don't help put Mama and Daddy ahead at all. 'Sides, I can't hardly breathe around here anymore!" Jurdine leaned. She never came around the bed; she never touched Hazel's cheek or took her hand.

"It would kill Mama and Daddy, Jurdine."

"But you know how it is! Look at what *you* did! It's either die or go crazy!" Jurdine was pleading with her. Hazel sighed, and despite the numbness, felt pain.

"I know," she said. She was so weary. "How come we can't be who we are?" she asked.

Jurdine's eyes flashed, and for a minute, she was not a ghost; Hazel glimpsed somebody she didn't know: she saw some kind of raven-haired queen.

"Nobody here *knows* who I am," Jurdine said in her old, high-and-mighty voice.

"*I* know!" Hazel said with all the energy she could muster.

"I don't wanna fight, Hazey," Jurdine said, half turning away. She stooped to pick up her pocketbook from the floor and then looked back. Before she could speak, the sounds of their parents' voices floated from the end of the ward.

"This is good-bye, Hazey!" she whispered. "I don't plan to be home when you get out."

Hazel was too full of everything to part her lips: fear, wonder, disbelief—she swallowed hard, and suddenly Jurdine rushed toward her and planted a hot kiss on her forehead.

"You always were prettier than me. That's why I hate you so much."

Hazel heard her sister lie to their parents about working a double shift that night. And then Jurdine was gone.

Johnson C. Johnson pulled over a chair and swung the curtain around the bed in one great swoop.

"Guess we'll have to put off our dancing, but not for long, I hope." JC wasn't smiling when he said it, and Hazel was strangely comforted by that.

JC sat down. He was clutching a bunch of purple hydrangeas, which made Hazel smile.

"You better stay out of Miss Clotille's backyard," she said, wanting to laugh but afraid it might hurt. "I believe she does count them blossoms."

JC cocked his head and laid the flowers on her lap, reaching into his shirt pocket for something.

"She invited me to 'em," he said. "And asked me if I was coming to see you. When I said 'yeah,' she said to give you this." He handed Hazel a small, light purple envelope. *Lavender*, Miss Clotille would have said.

Hazel started opening the envelope by slipping her little finger under the edge of the seal. Miss Clotille said that a lady should never rip open packages or envelopes.

"You know, Hazel, life sure is funny sometimes . . ." He hesitated. ". . . but I'm not laughing about it."

"What in the world are you talking about?" she asked, slipping one of Miss Clotille's perfumed notecards from the ragged lips of paper.

"Well, I saw your sister when I was on my way over here. And she saw me, too; at least I thought she did. But then she kind of looked right through me and just kept on walking."

Hazel sucked in a breath. He hadn't named names, but she didn't have to wonder which sister.

"W-where was she, exactly?" Hazel tried to keep calm.

He leaned toward her and lowered his voice. "Easing into the bus station. She was in traveling clothes and heels, carrying a little grip . . ." He was watching for Hazel's reaction. ". . . and she was going into the Colored passenger entrance, not that side service door, so I knew she wasn't making no deliveries for the plant."

"You sure were paying a lot of attention," Hazel said sharply, because she was secretly afraid that Johnson C. Johnson might be judging Jurdine, like she was right now. Hazel suspected that Jurdine's actions were simple practice for the way she would pretend wherever she was going. She had already chosen the new kind of air she was going to breathe. It didn't include anybody like JC, or Hazel, or even Mama Vee. Hazel shuddered.

"The way your sister looked at me, I had to pay attention. It was like she was daring me to say something—anything—but then I blinked, and she cut me a look like I was something dirty on the bottom of them high-heeled shoes!" He sat back in the chair with his hands on his knees, still staring at Hazel.

"You knew she was going," he said.

Hazel was crushing the lavender note between her fingers. Without answering him, she opened it. Her hands were shaking. She read the first line, hoping for a distraction. She found one.

> "My dearest Hazel: I was sorry to hear about your misfortune, but as you know, I have a busy household to run. I consulted with your grandmother, and have had to engage someone else. She is a quiet girl with a desire to serve. With a bit more polish, you would have had great potential in a domestic career, I think. I'm sure you will keep a good enough house, if you ever marry. Yours in friendship, Clotille Veatrice Henderson, Esq."

Hazel looked across at JC with wonder. "Well, I'll be. She fired me!"

"She did what?" JC's eyes flashed, and he half-rose from his seat. "I oughta—"

"You oughta nothing, Johnson C. Johnson. But thank

you for jumping hot on my account. Let me swallow all this for a minute."

Every woman in Hazel's life except her own mother had turned on her, shown all their ugly, and she wasn't sick over it. Hazel was surprised that with all this loss, her heart wasn't heavy.

"JC, you're so right!" Hazel said slowly. "Life is mighty funny . . . in that sad kind of way."

"I may not be sure yet who I aim to be," she added, "but I'm real clear on what I'm not. Are you?"

"Oh, I know you're gonna make it clear to me, Hazel Mozella Reed."

Hazel leaned to touch him. She was aching, hurting . . . but she knew she would heal. She let the purple notecard slip off the edge of the bed as she moved.

"You think there's a wheelchair around here somewhere, JC? Looks like sunshine outdoors. Could we go outside?"

He leaped up, grinning like he had that day—it seemed so long ago!—when he'd called to her over Reverend Clark's hedge. Song of Solomon he'd recited, Hazel recalled. She winced and eased back against the pillows, hoping that she wouldn't fall asleep again before he came back.

But her eyes didn't close. There was too much now to think about.

# Hanging Out His Shingle

Covington marked an *X* on the line next to his name. He guessed that this was not the time to let on that he could actually reproduce the letters of his own name in his own hand from his own knowledge. He read silently, not even moving his lips.

*Covington Markham, June 19, 1868.* He would never have written the last name, anyhow. After feigning concentration over that crooked *X*, Covington looked up.

"Well, congratulations, Covie. You're a mighty lucky Colored boy," the lawyer said.

Covington didn't even flinch; he'd learned long ago that Colored and pride didn't ride well together. Not the kind of pride that could cause him to lose a livelihood. He only ducked his head to give the impression of a respectful nod, a mannerism he'd perfected working at his uncle's knee.

"Thank you, Mr. Worthy."

"Elizear Markham has left you an unbelievable gift, I hope you understand. What are you going to do now?"

Covington raised his chin and looked directly at Worthy as he slipped the papers into the inside pocket of his Sunday suit. He did cut a figure, he knew; and because his uncle had made sure he kept out of the fields, his back and shoulders were straight as a board. He wasn't tall, but he was wiry, and quick-limbed as well as quick-witted.

Covington turned his hat between his long fingers, aware that his green eyes, set deep in the shadows of his almond-skinned face, were cautious. Covington and the lawyer both knew that the question was only a coded version of the challenge the man was issuing from his own, equally green, eyes. And they both knew that Elizear Markham had left Covington what he justly deserved. Covington finally spoke.

"Well, Mr. Abe, I guess I gonna hang out my shingle and open up shop!" Covington wickedly enjoyed lapsing into the southern intonation and vernacular that his uncle had beaten out of him.

Worthy raised his eyebrows, surprised for a moment, then nodded.

"I suppose you are going to try," he said slowly. He reared back, his hands clasped under his chin. "I suppose you are."

Covington clamped his hat onto his close-cropped auburn hair without smiling. He gave his breast pocket a quick pat, as a final gesture to the lawyer that he would do much more than try. He believed in himself, and now that both the deed and the fully executed will were safely in his possession, what Worthy believed didn't matter.

"Afternoon, Mr. Abe," he said cheerily over his shoulder. "Your shoes be ready day after tomorrow."

Covington didn't wait or listen for any answer. When he stepped out into the crisp September air, he was wrapped up in wash-worn muslin, lavender scent, and kisses.

Beesi didn't care much for public propriety. And Covington didn't care much for anybody now, except for Beesi. He laughed and gently pulled her away from him.

He wanted to run his fingers through her soft, thick hair, but if a Negro man and woman showed affection out in the street like this, it might draw some unwelcome attention. So he resisted, slipping his arm underneath hers instead, heading around the corner.

"What you gonna do now, Covie? What you gonna do now?" Beesi was breathless and insistent, as always.

Covie rued the long-ago day when Beesi had been dropped (or thrown—he never knew) on her head, an incident that had somehow left its mark inside her brain rather than outside. Near about every sentence was repeated, every instruction forgotten once and then carried out twice. But that meant when Beesi hugged once, she hugged twice . . .

"Gonna practice my trade!" Covie put a loving hand on Beesi's shoulder. When his fingers brushed against her sleeve and the detailed scar underneath, he held them there, directing his rising anger from the brand on her arm toward a hope, an anticipation, of his future fortune. Their future fortune.

"Let's go home, Beesi," Covington said. He picked up his pace, and very shortly the two of them were standing in front of the neat and narrow two-story clapboard building, which stood at the edge of what used to be a cow pasture when the town was new.

Elizear Markham had come from up East with his Quaker parents, who'd sold their farm and come South to try to preach the slavery out of the town. To make a living and set an example, Elizear Markham's parents had started up a shoemaker's business and hired—not bought—Covington's uncle to learn the trade and work for them for pay.

Uncle Jim had appreciated the value of his position, and over the years he bought his own freedom and that of his sister. Not long after she arrived from the plantation, Elizear's father died and left him the business. Uncle Jim's sister became Mrs. Markham's friend, companion, and partner in turning the pasture into a rich and thriving garden, from which they grew and sold the most sought-after produce.

When Elizear Markham's mother dropped dead from a stroke in the middle of the cornstalks, Elizear and Covington's mother consoled each other.

Covington was born nine months later as his own mother died, and Uncle Jim lied that the baby was his own from a failed union. People chose to believe it, though the fair-skinned boy shared no physical features with his black-haired, square-shouldered uncle.

Elizear Markham had left Covington what he rightly deserved.

At the door, Covington slowly turned the key in the lock.

"Oh, Covie!" Beesi whispered, passing across the threshold before him, "Is it ours? Is it ours for true?"

Before he answered her, Covington quietly closed the door, flipped the "Closed" sign and pulled the shade. Then he threw the hat off his head and whooped.

"God Almighty, Beesi, it is ours!" Covington never imagined feeling genuine excitement like this pumping through his veins. He could hardly stand still.

"It's somethin' wonderful," Beesi murmured, stepping lightly around the small outer room of the shop. She touched the handsomely crafted man's shoe on display in the window and then skipped around to the shining wood counter, which she'd polished but had never stood behind.

"Wonderful." She smiled over at Covington.

He let himself go and grinned back, grabbing Beesi's hand to lead her into the rear workroom. He went to the tall bureau in one corner and opened a drawer. Beesi watched quietly, intently.

Covington drew a metal lockbox out and used another small key on his chain to open it. He slipped his precious papers from his suit pocket and laid them into the box, clicking it shut and locking it again.

Before he'd lifted his hands, Beesi caressed his cheeks. She turned his face so that he looked squarely at her.

"I got a powerful love for you, Covie," she purred.

The next morning, when Covington blinked his eyes open upstairs, Beesi wasn't at his side. And he was sure it couldn't be much past dawn, but he smelled coffee. Some cloth was tacked up at the two front windows, and his faded old work clothes were folded neatly near the wall, alongside his only suit. He got up from the pallet they'd made with a couple of quilts and stretched.

A fine china pitcher and basin, each rimmed in blue, sat on a small table near the door. Covington at once recognized it as Beesi's wedding present from his uncle.

Beesi had already started the unpacking without him! Covington hurriedly washed and dressed and rushed into the other room.

"Mornin', Sleepy." Beesi had set Elizear Markham's round pine table with a steaming tin mug of coffee and a fork, both flanking a heavy ironstone plate piled high with fluffy eggs and a plump, browned sausages.

"Good morning, Honey-girl," Covington said. His mouth watered. He hoped Beesi would always be full of such wonderful surprises.

Elizear had not been keen on the match, though Covington had overheard his uncle's salty "Ain't none of yourn, Master Markham, and you chose it that way! Leave the boy to his heart." And the way he'd said that, Covington remembered, was the closest any Colored man could come to accusing any White man of anything. 'Course, they'd been way out behind the shed on the far edge of the property, tanning hides. But Covington knew courage when he heard it.

Besides, his choice of a bride hadn't been all that complicated.

When Beesi first came to work for them, neither she nor Covington had made sixteen years. She'd come to tend house and the garden, and she kept her deep, dark eyes cast down. She never spoke. Townsfolk said she was mute, and simpleminded.

But Beesi put that lie to rest one day—for Covington, at least—when a mouse had run across his foot near the woodpile. Covington had unfortunately never gotten over his fear of such, and he'd squealed, jumped, and thrown his armload of kindling higher than his head.

A laugh, loud and sweet and free as singing, rang out from the kitchen window, and Covington saw Beesi smiling directly at him.

"You funny, funny!" She'd laughed, pushing the window up so he could hear her clearly, then shutting it quickly. She held his gaze for a long while, until Covington remembered himself and began to gather up the wood to go on with his duties.

Covington believed he had loved her from then on. They had waited four years till the end of the War to marry, so they could do it legal. Covington's only regret was that his uncle hadn't lived to see freedom come—nor see them wed.

"Beesi, I thought we were going to set up house together today!" He gulped coffee sweet with honey.

Beesi looked at him with a schoolteacher's stern frown.

"Don't you fret none 'bout that. I'm gonna put everything good. You got feet to make shoes for, dontcha?"

She flashed him a dazzling smile, her dimples deep, and Covington knew right away that Beesi was well aware of the way she had twisted the old folks' saying about making feet for shoes. Making babies.

Covington blushed.

Beesi, still smiling, waved her apron tail at him as if to shoo him off.

"Gone work, now. Gone!" she cooed.

Covington pushed back his chair and swallowed the last of the sausage.

He felt he must've been walking on clouds, leaving his own wife to go into his own business on his own property.

Covington sat comfortably at his stool and took a moment to survey the shelves of lasts around the walls; many he had carved himself. He could almost see the faces of the people whose feet were modeled in wood. Mostly well-off, these were generations of planters, farmers, businessmen, and fine ladies that Elizear and his father before him had courted and kept satisfied by their exquisite workmanship.

Along the bench to his left, Beesi had neatly arranged his familiar tools in the order he liked: lasting pincers first, to shape the leather onto the custom-carved lasts; the small hammer next to the awls he used to pierce elaborate patterns into the leather of women's shoes; rubbing sticks to finish the heels and edges just right.

On another small bench to his right were several pairs of shoes in progress. A ripple of annoyance ran through Covington; he was behind, everything was behind, what with Elizear Markham's sudden taking sick (though he was close to three score), and then the trips back and forth to fetch Worthy, whom he only spoke to behind closed doors. And then the dying, and the funeral, and the disposing of the shoemaker's things . . . the one face-to-face conversation Markham'd had with Covington was minutes before his last breath: he had insisted that all his personal belongings, except the pine table and chairs, be sold at public auction two days after his funeral. And then he had said, as if Covington were not standing there beside him, "And to my son, I leave my business, tools, and good name." Elizear's chest had rattled one last time, and his eyes rolled sideways. Worthy bowed his head briefly and then buckled up his case. Beesi produced two coins, which she placed on the dead man's eyelids.

Covington had turned away to the window, vowing—not against a dead man's soul, but to the perfect rainbow of a setting sun and passing storm—vowing that he would never take the name of his father.

That was two weeks and a lifetime ago. Covington leaned over his progress bench to examine the tag on the left shoe of a men's pair. This was Worthy's order. Covington set to work.

He enjoyed the sounds of Beesi humming and moving in and out as she carried things off the wagon they'd driven over from their rented room yesterday. She never interrupted him, and he never interrupted her. When the sun fell in just the right place across the wood floor, Covington got up and went across the shop to flip over the "Open" sign and unlock the front door.

He brought in a selection of tools to do finish work as he sat at the counter.

Business was brisk; there were still condolences to receive (on the loss of his "master," which he didn't bother to correct, since the year on the great big calendar behind him clearly added up to five years past that day Lincoln had used the unbelievable word, "Emancipation"). There were old customers to reassure and curious new ones to entertain, including the silly young daughter of a local plantation owner who wanted dove-colored slippers for her wedding party of twelve.

Covington remembered his uncle's teaching well. He was clear, he was precise, he averted his eyes, and he never let them see him cipher.

Near the end of his first day in business, Covington looked up as the bell on the door tinkled. "Sam!" Covington put down the shoe he was working on and got up to greet the giant of a man striding across the floor with the traces of Africa still proudly bred and borne across his nose and mouth and cheekbones.

Sam was carrying a package wrapped in brown paper. "Cov! I come to give you business!"

Covington smiled and shook his friend's hand, shaking his own head at the same time. "Hard to believe, Sam. I waited, and I wouldn't even let myself hope, but . . ."

Sam slapped Covington lightly on the back.

"Quit that nonsense talk. You a free man, done inherited your—" he paused, cocking his head to one side. "—your blood papa's business. It's what he readied you for, what's by right any man's. Now come on here, and measure these feets for me!"

Sam lifted his pants leg. Covington looked down, then up. Sam jangled coins in his pocket.

"I come to be your first Colored customer! You gonna do me right?"

Covington was speechless, tongue-tied by joy and gratitude.

"Do who right?" Beesi peeked through the curtain of the workroom. "Sam! Vi come with you?"

"Naw. She want y'all to come Saturday night for some cake and good wishes on your fortune," he said with a straight face. "And I come to get myself measured for some of Cov's shoes!"

Beesi clapped her hands together, then propped them on her broad hips. "Shop closed, Sam. Shop closed. Covie done worked a full day, and friends don't get special!"

"Beesi!" Covington laughed.

"You got a tough biddy there, Cov!" Sam laughed too. "All right, I come reg'lar hours tomorrow, soon's I get off my job." He moved to tap the brown paper package.

"Meantime, this here's for you, Cov. Vi and me put our heads t'gether on it."

"Oh, open it! Open it, Covie!"

"Beesi!" Covington laughed again. Covington ripped the paper, and his eyes blurred for a minute as he read his name, painted in bright blue swirly script letters outlined in black. The sign itself was arched on top, sanded smooth and whitewashed.

"Oh!" Beesi breathed, tracing the letters with her fingers. "It's mighty fine, Sam."

Beesi could neither read nor write, so Covington read out loud.

"Covington's Fine Shoes."

"You hang your shingle out first thing," Sam said over his shoulder, not waiting for thanks. "Else, I won't be able to find my way to my new shoes. Haveta go barefootin'!"

Beesi giggled, and Sam's chuckle rumbled down the street behind him.

Pleased as he was over Sam's gift, something inside Covington made him wait until darkness fell, wait until he and Beesi had eaten their cozy supper, to set up the tall ladder and remove the black bunting from Elizear Markham's sign.

Sam had drilled the holes just right, so that Covington's new shingle fit easily on the big brass hooks attached to the sign pole.

When Covington climbed down, a sudden breeze came from nowhere, swinging the shingle gently.

"Some kinda sign that you gonna be all right." Beesi leaned in the doorway, framed by the glow from the gas lamp inside. Covington froze that picture of her in his mind, because although he couldn't see her features, her presence was strength, somehow . . . and that soft, pale light was like sun coming through night.

Covington's next day keeping shop was actually the end of his week, a Saturday, and since Sam and Vi were expecting them to make a party, he thought to work a little longer than usual. It wouldn't do to show up early and set Vi into a tizzy, so he and Beesi had decided that around nine would be right.

Saturday had been the busiest day he could remember in a long time, as word had spread about the wedding shoes, and the girl had actually been showing around the little drawing Covington had made. Beesi had to come keep order behind the counter as the steady stream of White folks poured in, along with a trickle of new Colored customers. Every now and then, in a lull between the commotion, Covington would hear her say, "Mr. Covington be right with you, please. Have a seat. Have some tea."

Tea?! Covington almost choked the first time he heard that one, but the people couldn't get over it.

Beesi had purloined Elizear Markham's mother's china tea set in all its gold-rimmed beauty before it went on the auction block.

The time flew, and when the last customer left, Beesi went to put the china away and prepare for the party. Covington, caught up in the work he loved, stayed at his bench until he heard the muffled chimes of the clock upstairs as it struck eight. He began hurriedly clearing away, and dropped his hammer. As he bent to pick it up, he thought he heard a noise outside.

Who in the world could that be? The closing sign had been hung since five.

He took his time, picking up this and that, as he made his way to the front. The shades were drawn, so he would have to go to the door to see what was going on. Certainly, he now heard somebody—more than one somebody—outside.

"Covington!" A rough voice that he did not recognize seemed to growl his name. Covington had never turned down a customer before, but he had seen Elizear do it, and he knew that there were some folk he would never work for, even for pay.

He squared his shoulders back and set his jaw as he unlatched the door and opened it, pulling it shut tight behind him.

The glare of torches almost blinded him and completely hid the faces of the small group huddled a few feet away.

Covington tried to shield his eyes so he could make out the figures, but the flames waved back and forth. As if these people did not want to be known.

"Store's closed, folks. Come back first thing Monday morning." Covington did not use his Colored voice.

"Who you think you are?" demanded a high-pitched, youngish voice.

Covington squinted, but the torches moved again. "Unless you're new around here, you know who I am. Covington. Born and raised here, learned my trade here."

"What you doin' running a White man's business like it's yours?" Another growl. Mutters rippled through the crowd. Covington felt them begin to move.

"I think you made some kind of mistake," he said calmly. "This is my shop. My property."

A stone flew over Covington's head and crashed through the store window. He jerked around, but it was followed by another, which caught him on his temple. He felt blood trickle into his eye. He clenched his fists, but didn't move. "Get off my property!" he called out.

"The problem is you niggers all a sudden think you good as us!" The high pitch was a nasty squeak now. In his mind, Covington knew he was better, always had been.

Covington raised his hands in an attempt at conciliation. "I don't know what your quarrel is, but if you would just leave me and my wife—"

"Your wife? You mean that half-wit from Dawson's place?"

Covington's blood quickened inside him, and he stepped forward.

A fist as hard a stone knocked him down, and he felt the blows all over him, heard more glass, heard snapping, splitting wood.

He twisted his neck, wincing as a boot tip landed in his ribs. He could see his shingle flapping in two parts, cracked raggedly from top to bottom.

WHAM! BAM! They were trying to ram the door. Covington managed to elbow away a body and get up onto his knees. Through the legs and in the flickering light, he spied a dropped club on the ground. He crawled toward it, his fingers taking hold just as somebody grabbed one of his legs, twisting it until the pop and the pain exploded in his thigh. But Covington swung the club up, landing a hit.

"BEESI!" he yelled blindly as fresh blood from some

new head wound ran into his eyes. He heard the heart-stopping crash of the front door, and he dragged himself, pulled himself toward the step.

The attackers had all but forgotten about Covington now. They swarmed past him, swinging the clubs, catching shelves and sending shoes flying.

Covington tried to look at the upstairs windows, but couldn't see.

He prayed that they didn't have guns.

Then an ear-bursting howl broke through the men's cursing terror, and Covington blinked to see Beesi in the doorway of the workroom, her eyes wide and angry, her black hair waving like a dark crown.

Covington closed his eyes. "Lord, don't let one of them have a gun," he prayed, then watched Beesi's arms swinging, flashing the blade of her garden machete in one hand and a heavy brass poker in the other.

"COVIE!!!" she screamed and ran forward, wearing her best dress, wearing her fancy Covington-made shoes.

"Look out!" somebody yelled.

Covington slumped. They didn't have guns.

"Told you! That Black bitch is crazy! Look out!" They were falling back, Beesi was flying toward them, and Covington was cheek-down in the dust.

High-Pitch was hanging over him again, his sour whiskey breath whispering. Covington willed his broken body not to flinch.

"Lookit you, crawlin' in the dirt . . . You ain't nothin',

nigger," High-Pitch said before he aimed one last kick to Covington's side.

All Covington heard after that, before pain shut his eyes, was Sam's booming command.

"Say it to a nigger who's standin'!"

---

"You're a mighty lucky Colored man, Covie."

Covington's eyelids were heavy, fighting his attempt to open them. He had to try several times, and finally he squinted into the brightness of midday.

He realized, as he shifted his body and felt pain answer back, that he didn't know just which midday it was. He had a dull ache on one side of his head, and there was some kind of binding around his ribs.

Abe Worthy was sitting across from him.

Was this a dream? Or a memory? Hadn't he heard those words a long time ago?

"I have to tell you, though . . . that wife of yours . . ."

Covington tried to push up at the mention of Beesi, and all at once the screaming and crashing of that awful night washed over him, pressing him back down.

"Beesi?" he croaked. Somehow, he couldn't make his voice any louder.

Abe Worthy leaned in and said in the same low tone, "She's just fine. I'm supposed to watch you until she returns."

Covington thought he heard wrong. He raised his brows in question. Worthy was smiling, shaking his head and looking off as if there was another life going on in the air between himself and the window.

"Your wife, Covington, saved your life. Oh, your friends came, and even a few of your sympathetic White customers were roused from their parlors. But they needn't have worried. She got at least one good wallop in on young Dawson with that poker. She shed no blood and scared them witless—if that, indeed, is possible. But then, I understand, she had your friends bring you up here, and she herself went to fetch Doc Barton. Don't try to move, now . . . I have strict orders from your nurse."

"How long . . . have I . . ." Covington coughed, and his ribs hurt.

"No talking, Covington, nurse's orders. Now, where was I? Ah, yes. I came into the story later that evening, when your wife bundled all your shoe lasts into a bedsheet and dragged them across town to my office, where she insisted that I lock them up in my safe. Then she informed me that I was to escort her, as soon as she 'did her hair up respectable,' to the sheriff's office to file charges for, as she so eloquently put it, 'outrageous damage to the business and body' of her husband . . . you."

Covington was not exactly surprised; he was more proud, in a way he had never been before, of the choice he had made. Of the woman he had decided to build his life with. He carefully turned his head to Worthy, wanting to know more.

"Yes, well, after that pronouncement, Adebesi proceeded to describe all seven of the White men in question in such detail that the deputy had to look for extra paper to write it all down . . ."

Covington forgot himself. "She told you her name?"

Before Worthy could answer, there were brisk steps in the stairwell that carried across the floor of the sitting room. The bedroom door was abruptly thrown open, and there was Beesi.

There was the sunlight smile that hurt Covington's eyes and healed them.

She took two steps in, and his heart began beating so fast Covington thought it might jump out of his chest.

"Thank you, Lawyer Worthy. Now Covie and me gonna be alone!"

Worthy bowed as he obeyed Beesi, turning to wink at Covington.

"I reckon I'll see you some other time, Covington. Miss Adebesi, whenever I can be of service?"

Beesi nodded curtly, and didn't even see the lawyer out. She shut the door behind him and walked slowly to the bed.

"How you?" she asked. She touched his forehead. Covington shuddered.

"Covie?"

"Fine. How are you?"

"Fair."

Covington grinned at her modesty. She looked

wonderful to him. He reached up and pinched the tip of her nose.

"Been busy, I hear?"

Beesi ignored him. "Time to get up, time to move." She bent to slip her arm behind his back. As he raised himself up, Covington was aware of a numbness in his left leg. He threw the covers back. Was it—no, his leg was there, laced to a thick splint. He tried to move it, and the numbness turned to throbbing, but he couldn't lift it.

"Doctor don't know, Cov. Said you gotta try. Maybe you walk like old times. Maybe not. Now, get up."

Beesi heaved, and Covington gave it his all, and he was standing, his arm around her neck. He was dizzy for a bit, but Beesi was perfectly still, as if she knew.

"I'm up," he said. She produced a cane from somewhere and thrust it into his hand, then slowly unwound herself from him.

"Try," she said.

Covington started with his right foot, then pulled his left leg along, feeling tingles from his thigh to his calf. His ribs hurt, his head hurt. Beesi walked backward in front of him. He sighed. She was going to make him go all the way into the sitting room.

Covington snorted. If she was going to be stubborn, he was going to be determined.

He wasn't sure how long it took. Sweat moistened the back of his neck; he was beginning to feel a little lightheaded. At the doorframe, he leaned to rest.

Beesi stepped to one side.

Under the front window was his workbench. Next to it was his stool.

"Come, come." Beesi took his hand and nestled close, almost like she was becoming Covington's left side. He sat down hard on the stool and swallowed as he looked down. There were his tools, placed just as he liked them. Lasting pincers, small hammer, awls . . . and tucked underneath one of the smoothing sticks was a scrap of brown paper.

Covington slowly slipped it out and held it up close to his face.

It was his sketch of the dove-colored wedding shoe.

"Beesi, I—" The emotion stopped him. Beesi got down on her knees and looked up into his eyes.

"She gonna wait. They all gonna wait, for Covington's Fine Shoes." Beesi squeezed Covington's right hand and drew the muslin window curtain back.

Covington saw his shingle hanging there, all of a piece, letters perfect and paint fresh. He grabbed Beesi's chin and kissed her, once, twice, three times.

"We've got a powerful love, Adebesi," he whispered.

"Powerful, Covington," she murmured back, brushing her lips against his eyes and forehead.

"We got somethin' powerful."

# The Season to Be Jolly

Girl! Put some more coal on that fire. I told you not to let it burn down so low. There's a chill in here! I don't want to look like a snow queen in my portrait. Hurry up, why don't you?" The plain young woman rustled only slightly in the direction of the little brown child in the corner of the room. The shining pleats of red silk that pooled around the young woman hardly moved.

The child blinked away sleep. She was so tired, she'd been dozing. It took her a minute to gain her senses, but she knew that her mistress wouldn't dare reach out to strike her. This time. She would never risk putting a hair out of place, not after the hours she'd spent carefully arranging her curls and painting her face for the picture-taking man.

And besides, he had said the mistress must be still as stone while he was preparing to make his exposure. But she could move her lips.

"Well? And can't you see that our guest needs some warm drink? You tell Annie Cook to send in a plate of sweets, too!"

The tall, red-haired man winked at the child as she jumped from the low, round stool where she was sitting. She took a chance and offered him a quick grin in return.

"How dare you get familiar with my company!" Mistress screeched, and a dainty pump flew past the child's head, almost landing on the hearth. The child darted her eyes to the fireplace, and the man laughed in genuine enjoyment as he bent to retrieve the shoe.

The child knew the mistress would take this as humiliation and make her pay dearly for it later on. It was almost worth it, she thought, crossing the soft wool carpet into the hall. That man had a laugh like music, and his eyes were like clear blue skies. She heard him speaking in low tones to the high squeaks of Mistress's complaints.

In the wide center hall, the child heard singing. It was an odd, welcoming thing, to hear singing in the middle of a December morning. Something made her bare feet move toward the front of the house rather than the rear, toward the kitchen. She drew back the lace curtain to see a group of people huddled across the street.

"'Tis the season to be jolly . . ." they were singing. The child pressed her small nose against the cold glass.

They were Colored people! She stared. They were Colored people, just like she was, and they had on pretty and plaid wool coats and bright hats and mufflers. They had smooth, full faces and nice eyes, and they were singing to her from across the street!

As the child watched, one man in the middle, a broad-shouldered, honey-colored man with a gap right between his front teeth—that man lowered his songbook and looked at her.

A sudden draft blew in from underneath the wide front door, and the child dropped the curtain in fright and shivered in her cotton shift.

The singing stopped, and she was sorry that it had ended. With one timid finger she lifted the corner of the lace and twisted her head to peek out.

The Colored choir was gone, and the slate walk in front of the stately house was cold and empty.

The child took a deep breath, wondering how a body could manage jolly when her life was just plain misery.

She rushed into the kitchen and set the heavy kettle on the front burner of the stove. She lingered there because it was warm.

"Girl! Ain't you got nothin' better to do than slouch front a' the stove?" Annie Cook stuck her wide, dark face in from the food pantry. The child could see a few tiny, shiny specks, like Mistress's diamonds, flicker on Annie Cook's cheeks. She was in there eating sugar out of a tiny copper pan.

The child turned her back, reaching into the glass-front cupboard to take out two pink Limoges cups and saucers.

Something hard hit the back of her head. Even with her cottony black hair standing every which way, she felt the blow. Her eyes stung with tears as the pan clattered to the floor. She looked around to see Annie Cook's empty hands and satisfied sneer.

"Sassy lil' heifer! You betta think twice fo' you open yo' mout' t' Miss Maddie!"

The child blinked through blurry eyes and carefully arranged the teapot and sugar bowl on the round silver tray.

Why did people around this house throw things? As long as she could remember (in all her nine years), one or the other person was always yelling at her, telling her to move faster, or listen harder, or do better. Nobody ever asked how she got the roses to grow taller than she was (she talked to them), or how she knew to put what book at Mistress's bedside (she'd taught herself to read them), or if she was too tired or too hungry to do anything (when she always was both).

She knew she didn't belong to these people—to the mistress, who was unmarried and unmarriageable. The girl had not belonged to the mistress's sad, sickly mother or her mean, rich father. There had been a brown houseboy, Jeff, who was older than the old man, and more sour. The girl remembered the way Jeff limped around on cold mornings, his leg stiff and twisted from an old fracture that never healed right. The young mistress had turned him out when her father died. Jeff couldn't stand females or children anyway. And Annie Cook was always too busy cooking food, sneaking food, or stealing food for her grown children to pay the child any attention.

So the child watched and listened and practiced reading in secret. She had no mother or father of her own, but she didn't belong to these people.

~

The child used to listen to the old man *pontificate* as his old man friends smoked and argued with him. She used to bring his newspapers and dust real slow while he exclaimed out loud to his wife who wouldn't listen about the world going to hell in a handbasket because Colored people had actually started turning out to vote.

He ranted because that W. E. B. Du Bois, "with his uppity light-skinned self," wanted Colored people to be worldly, and that other one, Booker T. Washington, "with the nerve to have the name of a patriot," wanted Coloreds to learn a trade and get paid the same as White men.

The child figured out that what made the old man mad was that Colored people *wanted.*

~

"It's about time!" The mistress had composed herself when the child returned. She was giggly and shy with the red-haired picture-taking man as the child placed the tray on a side table and poured tea.

"Say! Madeline, how about letting me take a picture of our little waitress here?"

The child felt a strange tremor run up from her heart to her throat. The mistress was silent, stunned by her guest's request. The child lowered her head and passed the photographer a cup and saucer.

"What is your name, child?" he asked in his direct, not-of-the-South voice.

"Girl," she whispered, not looking at him.

"Madeline?" he asked. The child looked at his shoes.

"Oh, I forget if she ever had a name," the mistress huffed. "She's just a girl. And I think you are perfectly ridiculous, William. Who would want a picture of a pickaninny?"

The photographer put his hand on the child's chin and made her look at him. She saw those eyes like skies.

"Let's clean her up, get her dressed in something presentable . . ." He removed his hand, almost respectfully.

"That is, if you'd like to be photographed." He was speaking directly to the brown child.

She looked at the mistress, a storm of pale fury in her holiday finery—and feeling frisky, almost cheerful—the child grinned back at the picture-taking man and nodded.

"Well! I am most certainly not paying for this, William!"

"Never mind. This will be art, and art is for the future; don't you know that? Now I know you have some of your childhood frocks that you just couldn't part with, selfish

Maddie that you are. Shall I . . ." He turned toward the hall and the stairs leading up to the mistress's boudoir.

The mistress popped up and grabbed the child by her arm.

"You shall not! Come, Girl." She dragged the child, twisting her arm, up the stairs.

The child didn't care, for once. Something had changed.

Keys clinked and locks clicked on the trunks the mistress drug out. She muttered and fussed to herself, of course, as she examined and tossed silks and linens and cottons onto the bed.

The child stood in the cold room, wide-eyed at the treasures.

Finally, the mistress stopped. A pale yellow cloud floated before the mistress's face for a second before she thrust it at the child and spun away.

"Hurry up! Don't make William wait."

The child hugged the dress against her body. It was really for summer, she knew, because it was cotton. But it had a sheen to it, so that as she moved in the sunlight, she could imagine that it was silk. After she heard the mistress's feet on the stairs, she went back to the trunk. There was a petticoat and there were stockings; there was a pair of shining black boots with a beautiful pattern pierced into the hardly worn leather.

She practically ripped off her shift; she didn't care, somehow. She took her time pulling on starched underpants and slipping the petticoat over her head. The dress had bell-shaped sleeves that stopped right at the child's elbow; ribbon was woven through eyelet holes all around their edges and tied into tiny bows.

She took her time and buttoned every button from her waist to her neck. There was a lace pinafore with a fine scalloped hem. She slipped on the stockings and buttoned the boots.

And then she turned to the tall looking glass and saw herself.

It was serious, her solemn brown face. Round at the chin and only a little wide above her brows. Even, smart eyes, she thought. Her mouth was kind of small. But her hair!

She patted it furiously, but it did not match the rest. She darted around the room, opening drawers and wardrobe doors until she found an old comb. She examined it closely to make sure none of Mistress's horrible long, yellow hairs still clung to its teeth. Then she combed and combed and parted and patted until the sides were all going down and there was a nice tuft falling to one side, just over her left eye. She pushed it up.

She opened the door with both hands and walked like a lady with small, deliberate steps. She ran her brown hand along the banister as she walked downstairs. She felt bright, like all the people in the Colored choir.

Something had changed.

"Damn you!" Annie Cook was hustling away the tea tray as the child passed into the parlor. The child jerked her head at Annie Cook and smiled.

In the back parlor, the mistress met the child's direct eyes with surprise. "Oh!" Mistress said.

"Come right here, I have a stool for you to sit on," said the picture-taking man.

"Girl, I'll have you know that as soon as this foolishness is over, you will remove that dress from your horrid little black body and wash it!" The mistress's voice was rising again.

"Smile," the red-haired picture-taking man told the child.

But she could not. She looked straight at the camera.

"Oh, William, this is so useless! She's nothing!"

"Now, you know there's going to be a flash on the count of three . . ."

"Miss Maddie, if that lil' heifer done tol' you somthin' 'bout me, she's a lie . . ." Annie Cook was hovering in the doorway.

"One . . ."

The child thought with longing of the Colored choir outside. Where had their beautiful voices gone?

"Two . . ."

She wanted, at that moment, with her whole heart, to *belong* somewhere.

"Three!"

She wished and she prayed her need with her whole heart.

*FLASH!*

The bright white light stunned her, and she fell off the stool. She felt herself tumbling, tumbling. It was surely taking a long time for her to land on the rug and find her feet! It seemed to the child that ages had passed before the beautiful boots were firm and flat on solid ground.

And there was singing again . . . it was a different tune.

The Colored choir had come back! But how could she hear them from the back parlor? The child was confused. She rubbed her eyes. She was no longer inside the wide front door. She was outside.

"What child is this . . . " the voices were singing. The child blinked. A group of colored people was standing on the street across from her. At first they seemed to be the same as before—joyful brown faces, bright clothes, welcoming voices.

Then she narrowed her eyes. The clothes were different . . . she could see some of the grown women's knees! And the noises around . . . automobiles like she had never seen before whizzed past. There were buildings in the distance with huge pictures painted on their walls. And those buildings! They were towers of brick and stone and glass!

She looked up high and saw bright blue sky.

"Honey, where are you supposed to be? Are you alone?" Someone was speaking kindly to her.

The child lowered her chin slowly.

A Colored woman and a man were crossing the street. The man had a curly black beard circling his honey-brown face. The woman had almost no hair at all, but she had glittering beads hanging from her ears, and her eyes were full of love.

Soon, the entire Colored choir had surrounded the child.

"You hungry?"

"Where are your people?"

"You must be freezing!" Somebody draped her shoulders with a soft purple shawl. The threads in it sparkled like diamonds. She felt herself grinning.

"We want to help you," the honey man said.

"This child is so beautiful . . . like a work of art! What's your name, Baby Girl?" The woman leaned to touch the child's shoulder, and when she did, the child knew all of it was real.

The brown child thought hard and then said in a firm voice, "Jolly. My name is Jolly!"

"*Tis the season to be Jolly*!" The Colored choir sang the same joyful song that they had in her old life, but this time it was just for her.

# Son's Story

## Part One:
## Jimmy Lee's Birthday

Jimmy Lee smiled at the birthday card signed with his cousin Son's boyish scrawl. "Crazy kid, can't wait to be a man," he chuckled and tossed the card aside. Then he slicked back his hair and looked down to check his shoes.

The shoes were brand-new two-toned wing tips. The softly pointed toes were ivory-colored calfskin, and gleaming red-brown leather—"oxblood," the salesman called it—spread across the instep like wings beating the sky on a cloudy day.

Jimmy Lee grinned at those shoes, straightened his skinny blue tie, and looked at the calendar from Harris Funeral Home that was tacked up on the wall next to the medicine cabinet.

It was not only his twenty-first birthday; it was Election Day, and he could vote for the very first time. Jimmy Lee had put in for the day off weeks ago, when he first found out at the secret meeting that the voting place was being switched. The Colored folk weren't supposed to know.

But Jimmy Lee's daddy, his uncle Booker, and a couple of the other Colored vets who'd come back after D-day with life and limb intact, well—they'd found out. And they were of a mind that a grown man who'd gone overseas and fought in muddy ditches for his country ought to have a say in picking out the next man to run that country.

Jimmy Lee remembered feeling so proud that night, watching his daddy's determined face shining in the glow from the flashlights.

"Please don't go," his pretty young wife begged as she walked in next to him. Jimmy Lee turned to look at her. Willa was the best choice he'd ever made, up until today. He smiled and touched her cheek gently.

"I gotta," he said.

She followed his long, lanky body as he moved out of the bathroom, through the kitchen, and into the front room that was their bedroom and living room altogether. They could really afford something a little better, since they were both working steady, but in this town, the only place for Colored people to live was this little huddle of shotgun houses set behind the gas station.

One day, Jimmy Lee told himself, he would do better than this. He would buy Willa the house she deserved.

He stopped at the crib near the window. Little Bernadette was curled up into a pink ball of nightgown and blankets.

Jimmy Lee was still amazed that he was somebody's father. And he took it seriously. He'd had some practice, looking out for Son, but he was already a knuckleheaded kid—not a sweet baby girl. Jimmy Lee had big plans for Bernadette, like her going to college instead of straight to work like he and Willa had. And traveling, and eating in fancy restaurants, and . . .

"There ain't nothin' else I can do to change your mind?" Willa stared up at him with wide eyes. He could see himself in those eyes; he could see himself inside the fear that was looking at him.

He shook his head. This time he didn't smile.

"There ain't nothin' else I can do, except this, to change it for her, Willa. You know it well as I do."

He opened the door and stepped out. He moved fast. The dirt road puffed up around him. He didn't notice the dusty powder settling on his shoulders and his shoes. He didn't notice because he was moving with purpose.

Around corners. Up the paved street. Onto the sidewalk. Past the post office, where the voting was supposed to be. Where the newspapers and radio said the voting was supposed to be.

He saw his father's fedora in the middle of the clump of brown-faced men stopped at the steps of the public library. Jimmy Lee saw two White men, both men he knew, both vets like his daddy, scowling down at the men from his neighborhood.

Jimmy Lee hurried to be a part of them.

"What y'all boys doin' here, Bernie?" one of the men called out to Jimmy Lee's daddy.

"We here to vote!" his daddy called back.

"You boys don't want no trouble, now." The other man folded his arms and moved real easy-like, blocking the door.

"We here to vote!" Jimmy Lee's uncle Booker shouted from the crowd. All the brown men began to make noise. A White lady stuck her head out of the library door, but quickly yanked herself in again.

"You musta got it wrong, Bernie. Ain't no Coloreds votin' here today!"

"That ain't right!" Jimmy Lee heard himself yelling.

Jimmy Lee shifted his weight from one foot to the other. He was getting mad, getting hot. He had waited for this day! Dreamed of it. He was a husband, a father, an upstanding member of his church. Willa had baked him a yellow cake with jelly icing. He had dreamed of all that.

And he had dreamed of entering his legal manhood by walking up to vote in his church suit and his brand-new oxblood shoes.

Yeah, Jimmy Lee was hot.

When the brown men moved forward toward the library, Jimmy Lee moved with them. He only faintly heard the screech of car wheels somewhere behind him.

But he did hear the unmistakable sounds of the shotguns being pumped. And there was all of a sudden a crash, like something breaking, and smoke rising up at the same time as a thunderous booming sounded behind him. Shots blasted against screams and running feet. One shot, two. Many.

Jimmy Lee saw his father go down.

For one crazy second, Jimmy Lee imagined the evening yet to come. He saw ahead to his family all around and pictured himself bouncing Bernadette on his lap and laughing at the grape jelly smeared all over her face.

And then he felt a strange, burning explosion inside his chest, and he was lifted, lifted into the air, right out of his oxblood shoes.

It was November 6, 1956. Jimmy Lee's twenty-first birthday. His last.

# Part Two: Father

The boy hung at the edge of the crowd, soaking up the energy thrown off by the fear and excitement of the moment. He followed the group of Colored men dressed to the nines and moving as one body, because he had no mother to beg or threaten him to stay away. The danger made his skin itch and tingle, but the righteousness of it, the righteousness of this march through the dusty streets of the unimportant Mississippi town, the boy never doubted. Thanks to his father, the boy's notion of justice was sharp as a straight razor.

Son had skipped school. On a different day, Papa would have whipped his behind for that, even though he knew his boy could already pretty well outsmart the poor, barely educated "teacher" that the White superintendent had hired for the ramshackle, one-room Colored school. Besides, the boy thought as he passed the deserted-looking town hall, he had a feeling that he would learn more today than he ever had before.

The public library was the place. The town didn't really have much of a main street to speak of. If you zoomed by in your car the way most Colored people had to, by the time you shifted gears to clear the hill and checked your rear mirror to see if you'd been followed, you were already on the other side of the lumber mill at the edge of the city limits.

A local politician had finagled state money to put in a dozen live oak trees to "beautify" the dull stretch, instead of demanding money to expand the mill and make more jobs. Papa said the man preferred to contemplate any kind of shade other than the shade of the skin of third of his constituents. Today those brown men rolling up the street had decided to open his eyes a little bit.

It was a dangerous business, trying to vote in this county—dangerous if you were Colored. Son himself had heard a man in the grocery talkin' all loud about how he would "*strongly discourage*" any niggras from showing up at the town hall for the governor's election last year. And a few years before that, a man down their row—you couldn't rightly call the badly built line of leftover sharecropper's cabins a street—had started up an NAACP chapter. He and a handful of souls, men and women, had been dragged out of their meeting and beaten like they'd stolen money.

Come to think of it, maybe that was how White people saw it, Son suddenly thought. A voting Negro might want a good job, too. And a Negro with a job maybe meant a White man without one. Papa had come back from the war to marry, and when Son was only a year old, his janitor's job was gone, his wife dead, and his eighth-grade diploma wouldn't get him full-time doing much outside the cotton fields. He was smart enough to capture six Germans by his lonesome and hold off the enemy for two days after his unit got routed, but there was no respect for him in his hometown.

Papa and Uncle Bernie and Cousin Jimmy Lee were determined to vote today because they said voting would change things. Voting made their voices louder without shouting, Papa liked to say.

"All I want is my due, Son. When you get to be a man, you deserve to get as good as you give. " He'd rubbed Son's round red head this morning and set out. Yes, Papa was brave through and through.

As the boy smiled to himself, a harsh voice whispered from the front porch of a house just across the street from the red brick building.

"Son Collins! Where you think you going? You better—"

He rolled his unblinking gray-green eyes. He was ten years old, not tall yet, but solid. Certainly he was a match for the shriveled dark woman in the stiff-starched maid's uniform, if she got a mind to try and stop him.

The fierceness of his look seemed to cut her voice. She mumbled, and he turned his head, intent on seeing the scene unfolding a few feet away. He only half-recognized her, anyway . . . most women had ceased to matter to him a long time ago. He even had difficulty recalling his mother's face now.

Over his shoulder, he heard the woman suck her teeth and growl at his back.

"Hinckty little yellow bastard. Y'all gonna end up seeing what's what!"

*Fool!* he wanted to shout, but he suddenly caught a glimpse of his father's bearlike body nearing the steps. Papa was in front, along with his brother-in-law Bernard and his nephew Jimmy Lee. Papa wouldn't let anything stop him. He was a born leader.

Son stepped quickly over to the nearest tree and shimmied up the trunk, stretching his body out along a sturdy branch. He scooted a bit and then had a clear view through the leaves. He heard himself panting and knew it wasn't from the effort of the climb.

The big oak doors of the library were opening, and two White men stepped out. At the same time, the brown men fell silent and moved more tightly together. Son glanced across at the second-floor windows and saw pale, painted faces and blonde curls pressed up against the glass panes.

A freckled man in a Panama hat moved down one step.

Son recognized him from the Veteran's Day parade—he'd ridden on top of a tractor hung with a sign that read "Sibley and Sons, Farm Equipment." He had grinned and waved and thrown penny candy.

"What y'all boys doin' here, Bernie?" he asked, as if it wasn't clear as day.

Uncle Bernard stepped away from the group. "We here to vote!"

Son's papa moved forward. The other White man folded his arms and stood straddling the door.

"You boys don't want no trouble, now," he drawled without dropping the cigarette from his lips.

Jimmy Lee and one of his friends began to make noise. Son could see that there were a good number of women in the group, too. They were dressed fine, fancy hats and all. Uncle Bernard and Papa were in the lead, shoulder to shoulder.

"We here to vote," Papa repeated. Son wished that he could see his father's face. Was he calm, or defiant-like? Had his nostrils flared wide, the way they did when he was about to jump hot?

The smoking man shrugged. "You musta got it wrong. Ain't no Coloreds votin' here today!"

"That ain't right!" Jimmy Lee yelled, pushing his way to the front. He was wearing his brand-new wing tips. Cream and oxblood. Jimmy Lee had let Son tag along when he went to the shoe store to buy them, and even asked for Son's opinion. Jimmy Lee was like the brother Son always wished for and never had. Jimmy Lee was a cool cat. He was out there, ready to take heat just so he could vote like a grown man. Son thought Jimmy Lee was brave, but he'd never tell him that.

Today was Jimmy Lee's birthday, and there would be cake and ice cream at his house tonight. Son had dropped off a card this morning on his way to school.

"We comin' in, Sibley," Jimmy Lee's father, Uncle Bernard said, and the Colored crowd surged forward. But Son was distracted by the hum of a car engine, a hum that shifted gears into a roar, and he leaned so close to the rough bark that it scraped his left cheek.

The dark Chevy barreled around the corner, heading straight for the library steps. Son hugged the branch, opening his mouth wide to holler, but time happened too fast. Time ran as fast as that car did, but the car swerved just as it pulled up even with the three Colored men in front; wheels screeched and drowned out the boy's warning, and his second call was blown back into his throat by the explosion and fire that leaped out of the passenger side of the car. Shots rang out in the smoke; women screamed and men ran.

The car pulled away as quickly as it had appeared. Son blinked down into the smoke as it mingled with gunpowder and burned up his nose. There was blood: on the steps, on the ground, on the street. Blood on the White men.

Blood was seeping out of the still bodies on the sidewalk. One was turned away. That must be Uncle Bernie.

One slim, young form was sprawled in the arms of Jimmy Lee's best friend, Marcus. Son leaned dangerously off the limb. Those shoes . . . That was Jimmy Lee! Son swallowed hard. Where was Papa?

A giant, bear-shaped figure was slumped on the bottom step, his arm stretched out. Was Papa making a fist? Or was he reaching for help? Son kept pressing his eyes together, opening and closing them, hoping to see something different. But the smoke was dissolving.

He raised his head. Across the street, staring directly at him from one of the upstairs windows, was a pink-faced woman with silver hair and lips the same color as all the blood. Her gray eyes were wide, meeting his.

She turned away.

Son breathed in and his chest hurt. Slowly, he climbed backward and made his way to the ground. He could hear the police sirens coming. He could hear panicked voices asking each other what happened. He already knew that there would be no answers. He already knew his father was dead.

He trudged along to Jimmy Lee's house and stumbled up to the backyard's chicken wire and wood post fence. As he climbed over he had the feeling that he was traveling through some kind of dream; the chickens in their nearby coop didn't even flutter, and though he came down smack in the middle of the vegetable plot, he barely brushed the giant clumps of collard leaves. At the corner of the garage he paused to wipe what he thought was sweat from his cheeks. He noticed a trickle of brown figures coming down the hill in front of the house, making a raggedy line in the direction of the front door.

Son realized that it had become Willa's house, and in one afternoon all the men left in his family were gone for good.

He spun around to the toolshed and pushed the door open. Then he sat on the cool dirt floor in the shadows and leaned his head back against the musty wall to wait.

Finally, the sun faded and Willa pulled the door open with a sudden jerk. He sat up just as quickly, bumping his head.

"Well," she said, her arms folded and her head tilted so that he could not read her features. He wondered if she did that on purpose. From now on, either everything had a purpose, or nothing did. "I'm not stayin' round here. Soon as I bury Jimmy Lee, I'm gettin' the hell out. You may as well come."

Numb as he was, dazed as he was, all he could do was shudder. Willa accepted that as a yes, and in barely two weeks' time, Son was a conflicted resident of Washington, DC.

# Part Three: Mothers

He was mad. He was ticked off. He was in a rage nearly every waking hour. Willa was only nineteen, hardly knowing how to mother her own baby girl and manage a job. Son was out of her league. His anger met her coming and going.

She put him in school, and though the teachers recognized his brightness the same as his father had, he fought them with disrespect. When Willa tried to talk to him or chastise him, he fought her with silence.

In the mostly White neighborhood of Anacostia the few Colored kids teased him for talking "country," for dressing in the too-small castoffs that Willa could afford, for having no mother or father or drive. He declared all-out war on them, throwing rocks and curses and punches.

Years slipped by, counted only by Willa's sighs and Son's detentions and suspensions. On the evening of his thirteenth birthday the DC police brought him home for vandalism with a promise to arrest him next time.

Son watched Willa slump on the front porch as she spoke to the cops in low tones. He knelt by the pallet on the floor where Willa's daughter Bernadette lay sleeping. He stared at her in wonder, the way he often did, and for a moment his nothingness took the shape of fondness. She smiled at him in her sleep.

How can little kids dream, he thought sadly, when growing up hurts so much? Willa had never shown him love. She shared her home and food and the little attention she had to spare, but she couldn't spare any love.

"Well."

He turned from Bernadette to face his new future like a man, because he knew that's what this conversation would be about.

Willa was tired. He heard it; he saw it in the haphazard way she pulled her frizzy brown hair back with a cheap rubber band. He saw it in her eyes: scared, somehow still not-quite-woman eyes. How could that be?

"I'm—I'm sorry, Willa!" he blurted out, and to his embarrassment, fat tears rolled down her face as she hugged herself harder.

They were family, he suddenly realized. The only scraps he had. Willa and Bernadette. And he had screwed it all up.

"I've tried, Son. God knows I have."

He dropped his head. Nothing had stung him so far in his battle with the world like her words did, because he knew she was telling the truth.

"Come on out back," she whispered.

He stumbled after her, into the tiny overgrown yard of the house she managed to rent. He tried not to see the scraggly pole beans in the weedy little garden plot. He thought of Jimmy. Uncle Bernie. Papa. He thought of Men.

I could've mowed the grass, he thought.

I could've kept her garden up for her, he thought. I could've tried.

"Son, I gotta tell you something." She looked straight at him. He could feel the muscles in his legs tighten, but he didn't run. What was the use?

"I can't keep you no more."

He nodded again, looking dry-eyed at his feet. Willa had run out of second-hand sources to keep up with his size twelves; she had bought these tennis shoes new.

"I just—I just don't have what it takes to raise you. I'm real sorry."

His lips quivered.

"And I—" She hesitated. There was a change in her voice. He heard *guilt.* He raised his head. The familiar anger suddenly began to roll around the bottom of his stomach like hunger.

"—I don't know how to say this, except to say it. Your mama ain't dead, Son. She never was. Your daddy and her brother, Jimmy Lee's daddy—well, they made it all up. To protect you."

He rocked, but his knees didn't bend. Willa put a hand on his shoulder. He wanted to shrug her off, but he couldn't.

"It wasn't right for them to lie, but they had their reasons, I guess. I kept it because it was their lie, not mine. People talk bad, and they don't forgive. They say she left him, left your daddy. Say she claimed she wasn't satisfied or some such foolishness. I can't even imagine! With a perfect baby child—"

She caught herself and blinked at him. "I don't know how she could ever leave you," she said honestly. "Maybe, most probably, you would have turned out different if she had stayed."

"Why? W-why—?" he stuttered, unable to get a complete sentence out.

But Willa nodded, seeming to understand anyway. "I'm tellin' you now, 'cause she needs to finish her job. You need somethin' I can't give you, Son. I'm tellin' you, 'cause I think your mama might be the only one who can help you see straight."

Son still couldn't speak. *Her job.* What was a mother who didn't want to be one? Just some woman. Just a quitter. She couldn't have loved either of them. And was his father a better man for hiding the truth? Maybe. But all his preaching about right and justice seemed kind of hollow in the light of this mighty wrong. Had he really been protecting his boy, or protecting himself?

Son blinked at Willa, empty. All his anger was gone. Nothing, not even hope, seemed to want to take its place, though.

Willa reached into the pocket of her maid's uniform and took out a neatly folded envelope and a bus ticket. He opened his mouth, then closed it. They knew where she was all the time.

He hated his father. He hated his uncle. And if Jimmy Lee had ever known anything about this, he hated him too. He set his face hard and forced his hand out to take what Willa was offering.

"I found her address in some of the stuff we moved with us. I wrote to her and asked her to come get you."

He unfolded the envelope. Willa couldn't love him, but she was kind. He was grateful, but he couldn't tell her. *2250 St. Bernard Avenue, New Orleans, Louisiana.*

"I told her your daddy died. I told her I was having trouble. It took a long time for her to answer."

Son slipped the single page out carefully, not expecting much.

> Dear Willa Mae:
> Just like Booker Collins to go and get himself killed over something like that, but I take care of my business. You may as well put the boy on the Greyhound. Here is a one-way ticket. He can call me when he comes into town.

His eyes blurred over the telephone number, going straight to the name scrawled crookedly after the brief, cold message: Trina Bayonne.

He'd discovered that he hated bus rides. He had seen and heard many things during the two-day trip, but he couldn't wrap his mind around any of it. By the time he stepped into the stifling bus station that smelled of crab legs and river, he could hardly breathe. It was the prospect of seeing her, of laying eyes on her, that tamped his feelings down and crushed his heart and lungs.

"Lord have mercy, you are his spittin' image." She was tall, big-boned, fair-skinned. Her bleach-blonde hair was Marcel Waved and swung at her neck when she moved. Her red lips seemed permanently puckered into a pout—or a kiss, but Son suspected the first. Her voice was low and growly. She squinted warily behind the hand-rolled cigarette that she held between her thumb and pointer, licking those pouty lips.

He stared back. What did she expect?

"I don't know what you expect," she murmured defensively, giving him the once over from his Willa-bought tennis shoes to the cap he wore over his badly cut hair. With a sudden, violent movement, she jerked it off his head.

"That's ugly," she said. "Ain't you got a tongue in your mouth?"

Son didn't wonder what she would be like. He didn't even wonder what New Orleans would be like, though he'd heard at school that it was a town of mystery and voodoo and never-ending parties. He knew everything he needed to know.

"You don't *know* me!" he said, watching her pencil-arched brown eyebrows rise as he spoke. He knew he sounded forceful. Sounded mannish.

She clucked, smiled a dazzling white-toothed wonder at him, and then looked off—maybe in the direction of their future, he thought. He was right.

"Boy, I *been* knowing you," she said. "That's why I wanted to get away from you. And your daddy. And my brother, Bernard. And that tired-ass Mississippi mess. Face it: what's lost is gone. I borned you, a fact that was my mistake. But like I told Willa, I take care of business. That's what you are. You gonna carry your ass to school, and get a job so you can pay for your keep. I got a life down here that suits me. If you don't suit me, little man, you ain't gonna weigh me down. You gonna get to gettin'. We clear on that?"

The thin trail of her cigarette smoke had floated away. Son shifted on his feet for balance. Then he reached and snatched his cap back, plopping it squarely on his own head. This is the moment, he thought. I could let loose on her, or I could . . . "I'm just biding my time," he said in a voice so quiet that he scared himself. He didn't know where that voice or those words had come from, but he felt that he meant them. And he wondered now what he had been fighting for, these three years. This? Not this. What had he dreamed of, those nights that Papa had told him nursery rhyme stories and slave stories passed over the years, tales of folks who had run *toward* something? He had hoped that all of it, some of it, was true. But had everything been a lie, including good and evil and the justice his father had died looking for?

"Ain't we all," she answered, turning away from him as if he was already forgotten. "Ain't we all," she repeated to herself as her heels tapped across the linoleum.

Son ceased to feel that first day in New Orleans. He became an observer, a witness.

~

She lived in an upstairs flat and said that she worked in a bakery on the night shift. Every afternoon she had two fingers of bourbon and a dash of Coca-Cola in a tumbler, and she showed him how to fix it. For a long time, he thought she lived like the nuns he saw when she made him go to the Catholic church down the street, but pretty soon he realized that every night wasn't a baking night—that she had songs to sing in the French Quarter clubs and the Ninth Ward dives. There were men to see and laughs and gifts to be had, none of which concerned him.

As soon as he knew his way around, he snuck out and followed her. He studied the many men she found useless, but lived off of anyway. He found out from the nuns how to get himself into their Catholic school on a scholarship, and he got himself a delivery job after classes to pay for his uniforms. He and Trina passed few words from one week to the next.

She bought him nothing and taught him nothing. But that wasn't completely true, he told himself one afternoon at the public library when he was sixteen. His mother had taught him that there was nothing any human on Earth had to offer that would hold him.

She taught him how to be self-sufficient and self-absorbed.

He had learned from her that there was no such thing as love.

Son thought he should tell her these things. He went back to St. Bernard Avenue. There was no need for him to rehearse the conversation in his mind the way he did those with the nuns and priests and his shopkeeper bosses; he wasn't worried about her reaction.

He saw her through the screen door. She sat in her silk slip on the back balcony with a halo of cigarette smoke surrounding her pin curls.

He made noise on purpose, knowing that she really wouldn't care if he suddenly appeared. But he was self-conscious. He had grown taller, more muscular—he'd also found an interest in boxing and squeezed in time at the

Golden Gloves gym. He'd already been with half a dozen Catholic girls from school, but learning to make them pant and squeal had only confirmed his low opinion of women. The Young Saints Society was running a lottery to pick which girl would lay with him next. He would have felt sad for them, if he could.

"What you doin' home?" she lisped with the fag between her lips. He noticed that her creamy cheeks seemed to sag a little and that there were crows' feet radiating from the corners of her eyes, even though she had on full makeup. She always managed to wear full makeup, as if she was born with it on. If he had believed that it could be true, Son might have imagined that raising a teenage son was aging her.

But she'd had no part in it. He had a flash of Willa's worn brown face, and a twinge of something wrenched his stomach. It passed.

"I'm ready to go," he said. There was the slight sound of her newspaper crinkling. She took out her cigarette and slowly, deliberately, flicked ashes off the porch rail.

"What's that got to do with me? You ain't askin' for no money." It was a sure statement, not a question. He stepped to look over the rail, not at her. He could see the ashes, a tiny, smoldering mound in the withered grass below.

"I want you to sign me up for the army."

"They fighting a war, you know."

He spun to look at her—was that some kind of feeling? She was squinting at him, the way she had the first day they met. Her face was red. Maybe she'd had bourbon early; it had happened before.

"I know that. There's nothing for me here. And I want to go to school. The army will pay for it."

"If you live." She tossed more ashes. Her puckered lips worked silently, as if she was trying not to say something. Son had never seen this before. What had she ever hid from him? "High-minded Negro. Just like your daddy."

He frowned. Booker Collins had worked in the cotton fields, gone to the Second World War, and come back to more cotton. His highest aspiration had been to get a low-level job at the lumber mill, paying by the hour instead of by the pound. He had died trying to vote to keep the mill from moving to the White end of the county and successfully icing out most of the Negroes in their town. He'd been a quick thinker, a smart man, but never a learned one.

Trina scraped her chair back and stood up. He could look down on her now, and he did. They didn't like each other. Even so, he would not choose to change the last few years of his life. Maybe he was crazy. Son rolled his shoulders and flexed his biceps the way he did at the gym to show off, and smiled.

"Listen, you arrogant . . ." She paused, a first. He thought with amusement that she desperately wanted to use the word *little*, but even she knew that would not only be ridiculous, it would dilute whatever point she was trying to make. ". . . you arrogant yellow bastard." She was beginning to breathe hard. He had heard her recently, in her sleep, racking and coughing.

"Yellow?" He couldn't help the laugh in his voice, looking at her nearly pass-for-White face.

She raised her chin. He could tell right away that there was something she'd held back, something she'd been waiting for just the right, terribly right, minute to say. He remembered the day Willa had told him about her, and his senses went on alert. His knees locked. This time, his fists clenched, too. All at once, he was afraid that the dam he'd built against rage and desperation and longing might burst. He bit the inside of his mouth and felt the blood. He imagined it flowing, the way the life had flowed when he was ten years old. The bloody taste, bloody memory, comforted him.

"Booker wasn't never your father."

He stumbled backward, weaker now than he had been the day he'd stood hard and tall to Willa's confession. He grabbed the porch rail to keep from going over. His stomach rolled, and the mayonnaise sandwich he'd had for lunch turned sour and liquid inside him. But people had always said, "You're his spittin' image!" She'd said it herself! Now he realized that she'd meant something else entirely. His eyes widened.

Trina misread him for the first time, and she backed away as if she thought he would strike out at her. "I only married Booker 'cause that was all there was for a woman to do. I liked his looks, but I never was faithful, and he knew that. And then, early on, I ran off here and I stayed a couple months. I met a man."

Her eyes became dreamy, and Son was more upset than ever. Before she said the next words, he felt them. "*I loved him*. I found out I was pregnant with you, and I wasn't never going back. He was beautiful. Yeah, him and Booker—they favored—could have been brothers, I guess. Strange luck, things turnin' out that way... But *he* was different. He studied music and wrote his own. Was a horn player. He knew how to treat me gentle. Wasn't no roughneck cotton picker, and he never got mixed up in no politics. We were goin' on the road together..." Her eyes cleared, and she was staring at Son. "He got caught between two punks in the club where we worked and ended up cut. He bled to death in my arms."

Son swallowed. There was blood everywhere.

"They took him from me!" she shouted. "And I had to go back! Then you come, and every time—every day—I looked at you, I saw him! I couldn't *stand* you." She began to sob, and her cries became great, heaving gasps. Son mechanically took her hand and led her inside, where she hung onto the edge of her bed, shaking.

He leaned against the wall, sure that he would fall otherwise. She never said that if his father had lived, everything would have just been all right. She wasn't crying for the baby, the little piece of love that she could have even right now.

He wondered if Papa—Booker—had known the truth, but he didn't ask.

"I'll . . . take . . . you," she panted. "First thing tomorrow. First thing. I want you the hell out of my house." She looked at the floor.

Son pulled himself up straight. Even if she backed out of it, he would have to leave here. There was no way he could stay in sight of this woman and manage it; he knew that soon the fury would come exploding out, and something bad would happen when it did.

He wanted to hate her, but she had loved his father. He wanted to hate the man who'd raised him, but he had loved him. The world was cruel, the way it twisted regular people into monsters.

He walked past her to the front bedroom, began to throw all his belongings into a bag, and then thought: what do I really have? What do I own?

Nothing.

He went back to Trina's door.

"What was his name?"

"Absalom," she said.

# Part Four: Absalom's Birthday

The bus doors wheezed open in front of a dilapidated gas station and Son stepped out, wearing his crisp soldier's uniform. After ten years, he was seeing this world through a stranger's eyes. He began to sweat in the scorching sun, but he remained erect, bronzed, and proud and out of place in this Mississippi hamlet.

The few White people on the street stared through him. He was a nobody, even with the Purple Heart casting a glare and his shrapnel-shattered arm cradled in a sling underneath it. A Black man passing in a beat-up Ford honked and waved, but Son had never seen him before.

He shifted his duffel on his good shoulder as he walked,

noticing that the street was paved now. He squinted at a supermarket that seemed to have sprung up just to confuse him; a few strides more and he stumbled. A sidewalk had materialized. He glanced down in annoyance at his scuffed boot, and when he raised his head to the shimmer of heat surrounding the red brick building across the street, some of the first memories that he'd sent to hell materialized too.

He was standing right in front of the library. He looked immediately to his left for the live oak he'd climbed, but it was no longer there.

The library had expanded, and connected to the original building was a low-built concrete and glass wing with a sunny-looking entrance. He blinked at the old brick structure again and saw that it had been disfigured: the original awful steps had vanished; there was a series of windows in place of the wide wooden doors, and the grass and shrubs looked like they'd been growing there forever.

No sign of the murders remained. His brain understood it, coming fresh from killing fields as he had, but his being did not. If he hadn't been a man, he would have screamed. What had they done here?

He forced himself to cross toward the two slim young trees flanking the walk up to the addition. Each tree shaded a cast iron bench. As he approached, he looked inside the huge windows to see a group of very young children in a reading circle. Their cherubic faces were animated as they listened to the woman with cat eyeglasses and soft blonde hair. A few yards past them, half-hidden behind a row of books, he could see the dark figure of a young woman, her head cocked as if she was listening, too. Her mop and bucket were still, and Son wondered if she was frowning in concentration so that she could hear the whole story word-for-word, the better to go back and tell her own children. Certainly, they would never be allowed in this wonderful place.

He blinked his eyes against the scene and sat down on one of the benches. Newness could never hide the truth, or hide evil, could it? He slipped the duffel off his shoulder.

This was all old, so old. The men who had died here, men that he'd adored, had fears and failings and secrets that hurt him to the quick. But that pain was old now too; only a nagging ache remained. And though since his discharge a part of him missed the ever-present danger and the explosive relief he'd found in killing, living such a life had grown old as well.

He was back to nothing.

Trina was dead. Her downstairs neighbor knew he had gone into the service and took it upon herself to inform the US Army. In a cruel twist, Trina Bayonne had been found stabbed. He didn't know any details; he didn't want to know. He had refused the leave they offered him and gone on to rout a nest of Viet Cong that night. He'd killed them all.

Willa had dutifully answered the half-dozen letters he'd written over the five years, but he could tell she was trying not to promise him anything, and he understood.

Bernadette had colored a picture of herself and sent it once; he'd worn it inside his helmet and now carried it in his wallet. One of his buddies had joked about it being a love letter, and maybe it was.

What had Papa said one time? "You deserve to get as good as you give." Well, had Papa deserved Trina? Had he deserved to be shot like a rabid dog in this street? Son clasped his hands between his knees, not intending to pray, only to search himself. And what have I ever given anybody? Maybe that's why I haven't got a thing right now. Nobody and nothing to come home to. What did I give, except for arrogance—yes, arrogance, like everybody said over and over—and anger that bordered on crazy?

He had been washed in blood his entire life. He had survived all of it. So he must have a purpose. Maybe newness couldn't hide the truth, but what if the truth was faced up to? What then? Couldn't he be born again?

The real truth was that nobody in his life had ever had a fair chance. Maybe he hadn't either. It was time to stop running from that. Time to leave the bloodshed behind.

He spread his hands out to look at them. They were big, suntanned, strong. With those hands he could wrestle evil. In that moment of clarity, Son knew that from now on he would fight for anybody who wasn't strong enough or loud enough or mean enough to grab what the world owed them. He would give his whole self to this new fight, and he was determined that he would win. He could win. Son felt sure that he could fight for everything the men he'd loved had died for. They'd never had a chance. Son suddenly realized that Jimmy Lee had been the same age as he was now, twenty-one. He smiled to himself and sat back, reaching into his breast pocket for the bus schedule.

The buddy who'd laughed at Bernadette's crayon drawing, Joe Timmons, had actually been a cool kind of cat, from some little Louisiana town that sounded like a sneeze—Chabot. And he was going on about the Negro college his father had attended, some place called Grambling. "Coach Rob would lose his mind to get a bear like you on defense, man!" he'd said.

There was a bus to Shreveport. From there he had to transfer: Grambling was a town all by itself. Imagine that, he thought. A college town made up of Black folk!

He looked at his wristwatch. He had bided his time.

With his head held high, he got up to take a walk. Beyond the four main blocks the road forked. He didn't know where the right ribbon of dark asphalt led—but he knew the hill to his left. He strode over it, passing the ghostly lumber mill. The faded black and white sign hung crookedly on the padlocked gate. He wondered briefly if the politicians had succeeded in moving it, or if it had simply failed.

He continued slowly downhill. The remains of this deserted community were vaguely familiar. To one side was a weedy lot. The house where he'd been raised had once stood there. Nearby had been Willa and Jimmy Lee's place. It seemed there had been a fire, and only the ruins of the crumbling brick chimney crouched in the undergrowth, Jimmy Lee's shed having long ago tumbled down. The other shotgun houses on the row were only skeletons of their former selves, abandoned by the other broken people who must have left after Willa did. There was nothing here. Even the houses were dead.

He walked briskly back through his past, marking nothing to memory. His starched uniform and medals allowed him to step into the tiny store attached to the gas station to buy a sandwich and soft drink without incident.

He stood alone in the sun as the dusty bus screeched to a stop. The driver nodded at his uniform, then at him.

"Welcome back, son."

Immediately, the young man reminded himself that he had chosen to step into a new world. He had chosen to begin.

"The name's Absalom," he said smoothly, glancing down at the black block letters on his nametag. "Absalom Collins."

He would keep the fathers—the one he'd never known, and the one he hadn't known long enough. They were a truth he could never deny.

The driver smiled and accepted his ticket. Absalom Collins shook the clay dust from his boots before he dropped his duffel in the front seat facing the windshield and sat down, his eyes wide open for his new self.

# The Time Pamela Ann Got Kicked Out of Catholic School

The brown child squirmed in the hard wooden chair, trying not to look into the nun's disapproving face. She tried staring at her own black and white oxford shoes, with their double-tied laces that she had done herself. She tried a darting glance out of the big open window, but there wasn't even a cawing blue jay in the trees to hold her attention. Somehow, Pamela Ann couldn't help it. Her eyes were drawn back to Sister Formidable's eyes; they were angry dark beads.

"Sit up straight!" Sister Formidable barked in strangely accented English as she scowled over her eyeglasses. She rifled through the papers on her desk. The sound of the rustling pages swelled to fill the empty air, then stopped. For five long minutes, she pretended to read.

Across the desk, Pamela Ann became still. Calm. Sister Formidable wanted her to be afraid, but without the nun's words squeezing her heart, the child relaxed. She breathed slowly and easily along with her own *thump, thump, thumpety thump*. She wanted to smile, but didn't dare. Noise was the enemy, but silence? Silence was her best friend. That was why she liked to pray inside her head, *Blessed Mother, watch over me*.

Pamela Ann thought about Sister Formidable and her sister sisters. They didn't appreciate any honor to God that could not be heard echoing off the vaulted ceiling of the chapel or seen in the bent and scraped knees peeking out from the hems of navy pleated skirts—and if knees could be seen, that was another problem altogether.

Clearing her throat, Sister Formidable signaled that this particular period of punishment was over.

Pamela Ann allowed herself to sigh, acknowledging that her precious little spell of peace had ended. She waited.

"If the pagans were not in your home, you would behave like a good girl," the nun said carefully. Still, to Pamela's ten-year-old ears, she sounded as if she'd pronounced *g–i–r–l* as "gehl." And the pagans . . . Well. The pagans were Pamela Ann's grandparents and her father, who were Baptist. They were the ones who owned the business that paid the tuition for her to attend St. Benedict the Moor School, because her frail, "not quite right" mother had been a devout Roman Catholic before she got sent to the asylum in Pineville.

"I do not see," Sister Formidable continued, "why you felt you had any right to interrupt Sister Contumelia during a lesson."

"She said the '*niggras*' in this country should stop causing trouble." Pamela Ann repeated the pronunciation she'd heard as accurately as she could.

Sister Formidable picked up a ruler and rapped it on her desk impatiently. "What nonsense are you speaking?"

"Well, my mama says every one of us should protest for equality. And I told Sister Contumelia she said it wrong. It's pronounced *Nee-gro.* I know, because my mama taught me that, too." One of the things Pamela Ann had inherited from her mother was speaking things plain.

"Your mother, who is in the insane asylum! How dare you take this attitude! You are arrogant and disrespectful!" Sister Formidable spoke harshly but was apparently a bit flustered.

Pamela Ann had a delayed reaction to Sister's threatening tone. On any other day, that red-faced frown would have her squirming as she anticipated a fiery lecture accompanied by the burning blows of the paddle on her behind. But unfortunately for Sister Formidable, she had started Pamela to thinking about her mother.

There had been good times, fun times, before her mother went away. Everybody in Lowtown, where Pamela had lived all her life, said that Joyce Farmer was brilliant. There was nothing she couldn't do. She had learned to read when she was three and taken to the piano, playing by ear, shortly after that. They said seven-year-old Joyce quizzed the preacher about why God had put Jonah in that whale, and whether God had trapped Colored people on Earth for the same reason. She started following the Catholics after that. She was pretty, too—brown and slim, with flashing dark eyes and a heart-shaped smile. She fell hard in love with Beamon Toussaint, and he followed her off north to the university.

Something happened to her there.

The way Pamela Ann always heard her grandmother Ma T tell it, something happened, and when they came back south a couple of years later, Joyce wasn't the same. So she had borne Pamela Ann and lavished all her attention on her "little brown baby with sparklin' eyes," reading her Paul Laurence Dunbar and Dorothy West, Langston Hughes and Gwendolyn Brooks. She was thrilled by Pamela Ann's perfect pitch and sat the baby on her lap to reach the piano keys. In her mind, Pamela Ann could summon her mother's throaty voice any time of day.

Joyce went to Mass every Sunday and fell to her knees on Saturday afternoons in the confessional, staying for what seemed like hours as Pamela Ann sat waiting in the drafty, dim church, inhaling the sweet incense. What, the little girl had wondered, could her mother have done that much sinning about?

When Pamela was eight, she got tired of listening to the old ladies whisper with Ma T every time Joyce quoted Shakespeare or broke into a made-up opera about Negro rights. She got tired of watching her father's shoulders beat down during family dinners about "all his promise gone." He would only look at Joyce while she cocked her head back at him, smiling sweetly.

"Well, what happened up there?" Pamela had mustered up the courage to ask between bites of smothered pork chop one Sunday afternoon.

With a cool voice, Joyce had answered, "the white people killed your mother."

Ma T dropped the gravy boat. Grandpapa and all the aunts and the preacher fell silent as Beamon reached out and took Joyce's hand.

"She doesn't mean it, Pam," he said. But Joyce batted her eyes and nodded her head.

"Oh, yes. Yes I do. Pamela Ann, the White folks killed Joyce Toussaint. Your mama is not the woman she once was." She slipped her hand away from Beamon's. "Isn't that right, honey?" she asked softly.

Pamela Ann's father looked into his wife's eyes, then into his daughter's.

"You always was too smart for your own good," Ma T muttered, mopping gravy off her lace tablecloth. "Went up there and them White folks drove you crazy. She don't need to be left with Pamela, Beamon!"

Pamela's mouth had dropped open, her father abruptly stood up, and her mother screamed.

"You can't separate me from my child! She's the only way I'm alive! Beamon, tell her!" Joyce's voice rose hysterically, and she turned to Pamela. "Every time I look at you, Baby, I see who I used to be. Don't let them kill you too!"

"That's enough," Beamon said gently. But Joyce was shaking as she looked around the table for some agreement, some support. Pamela could see that it was only her father and herself who backed her mother up. She stood up and took her mother's hand.

Pamela remembered her insides quaking and barely holding the strong urge to let all her water out.

Suddenly, Joyce's knees bent, and as she sank to the floor, her face was wet with tears.

"Oh, I forgot," she whispered, almost to herself. "I'm dead."

~

Pamela had let her eyes gaze down at the shiny wood floor as she recalled these things, but now she slowly raised her head. She looked under her eyelids at Sister Formidable, and instead of a smoking behind, she felt hot anger inside.

*Arrogant and disrespectful.* She knew what arrogant meant—how dare this person talk about her mother as if she was crazy? Wasn't that disrespectful? And what did she know about real life anyway? That's what Ma T always mumbled about the nuns.

In first grade, Pamela Ann had thought they were holy women, the real wives of God. They were smart, they prayed, they spoke Latin and sang—almost like her own mother. But as she got older, she listened and she watched and she thought.

They were not always kind. They were not always generous. And sometimes—sometimes, they treated their little Negro students with the same roughness that they did the secondhand textbooks that St. Benedict inherited from the White Catholic school across town. They often treated their Negro students not with joy, but as if they were a penance.

Penance was what Joyce was always seeking in that confessional; penance was what the priest always gave Pamela Ann on Fridays when he chanted behind the red velvet curtain: Five Our Fathers. Five Hail Mary's. Pamela Ann's sin was always the same: she was mad at Ma T for sending her mother Joyce away.

Pamela Ann narrowed her eyes as she tried to look deep into Sister Formidable's mind. Past her horn-rimmed glasses, underneath the white wimple and black veil. She leaned to the edge of her chair, craning her neck.

Sister Formidable dropped the ruler and arched back, as if she thought Pamela might fly at her. Her blue eyes widened, and she went very pale.

Pamela Ann could hear her mother's voice inside her head. She smiled.

"I think—I think you owe my mother an apology... Sister." She slid back.

Sister Formidable's fingers crept to the black telephone at the corner of her desk. She attempted, but found that she was not able to dial a number while keeping her eyes on Pamela Ann.

A funny thought crossed Pamela Ann's mind. *Maybe she's afraid that I'm crazy!* The girl giggled. Sister Formidable fumbled through a small file of cards near the phone and then dialed with trembling fingers.

"I need Beamon Toussaint," she almost whispered. But she seemed to be recovering herself. "Yes, I mean *Mr.* Toussaint!" she barked, and waited—not looking across at Pamela Ann. "Beamon, you must come and get this girl. No, I cannot explain. She *must* go."

Pamela couldn't make out her father's muffled words, but the nun's fingers tightened on the receiver.

"I . . . I don't know about that. Yes. I see, but you'll have to take that up with Father—Oh. Yes, I understand—good-bye." She hung up in a rush.

"Should I go get my things?" Pamela Ann asked, swinging her legs under the chair. But Sister Formidable shook her veil vigorously and stood up.

"You will not return to Sister Contumelia's classroom; it would be too disruptive. I will gather your belongings and speak to your father. You will meet him outside . . ." She walked briskly toward the door, then paused with her hand on the knob.

"Pamela?" Sister Formidable looked over her shoulder. Pamela had never before seen such a curious expression on any nun's face. Was it wonder? Astonishment? A puzzlement that prayer might not work out?

"Yes, Sister?" Pamela Ann answered sweetly. Her mother was inside her, for sure.

The nun shook herself and blinked, as if she expected to see something or someone different when she opened her eyes again.

"Nothing." She clicked the door shut between them.

Pamela Ann smoothed the pleats on her skirt and wondered what her father had made the nun understand on the telephone.

"What possessed you, Daughter?" Beamon was leaning against the passenger-side door of his shiny gray Buick with his arms folded.

He didn't seem, to Pamela Ann, to be particularly angry or surprised. In fact, she thought as she slowly walked down the wide brick steps of St. Benedict the Moor School, he looked like he was proud.

Pamela shaded her eyes from the noonday sun and peered at him to make sure.

She had never lied to her father.

"Mama did," she said, stopping just a few steps away.

"I see." Beamon glanced away from her for a minute, then paid close attention to the filtered cigarette that he pulled out and lit.

"You know," he said, tossing down the burnt match, "your grandmother is worried about you."

"Because I got sent away from school?" Pamela Ann asked.

"Because you seem more and more like your mama every day," he answered, blowing off a series of round puffs of smoke. Each one was smaller than the one before it. Pamela Ann lifted her head to watch them float up into the sky together, joining the clouds.

"You're a lot like Joyce," Pamela Ann's father said in a funny voice, almost like he was talking to himself.

She looked in his direction, but he had turned to open the door for her.

"All that promise gone," he muttered, closing Pamela Ann's door with a soft click. She stretched up to see him through the rearview mirror as he came around the car. When he got in, he paused before he put his key in the ignition.

"What is it, Daddy?" Pamela asked. Her heart started beating fast, faster than fast, the way it did on the big Ferris wheel at the state fair. The way it had when she watched her Daddy drive off in this same Buick with her mama in this seat.

"Y'all both deserve better," he said firmly. He turned the key and shifted gears. And then he smiled at his daughter. "This place can't hold you, Pamela Ann."

Pamela sucked in her breath, not knowing exactly what was coming. She gripped the soft leather seat and stared over the dashboard. Her father didn't turn at the corner, heading toward the white-columned funeral home where

Ma T and Grandpapa ruled the same way Sister Formidable did at St. Benedict the Moor School.

No, Beamon cruised through the town, going somewhere else. He left the city limits, sailing on the blacktop toward the highway turnoff. At the flashing red traffic signal he slowed to a stop. Pamela Ann's heart was in her throat.

"Daughter," he said, taking a deep breath, "we are breaking out."

He revved the motor and put the car into drive, screeching left past the sign that read *Pineville, 49 miles.*

With her heart thumpety-thumping again, Pamela Ann sat back to enjoy the ride.

# A Matter of Souls

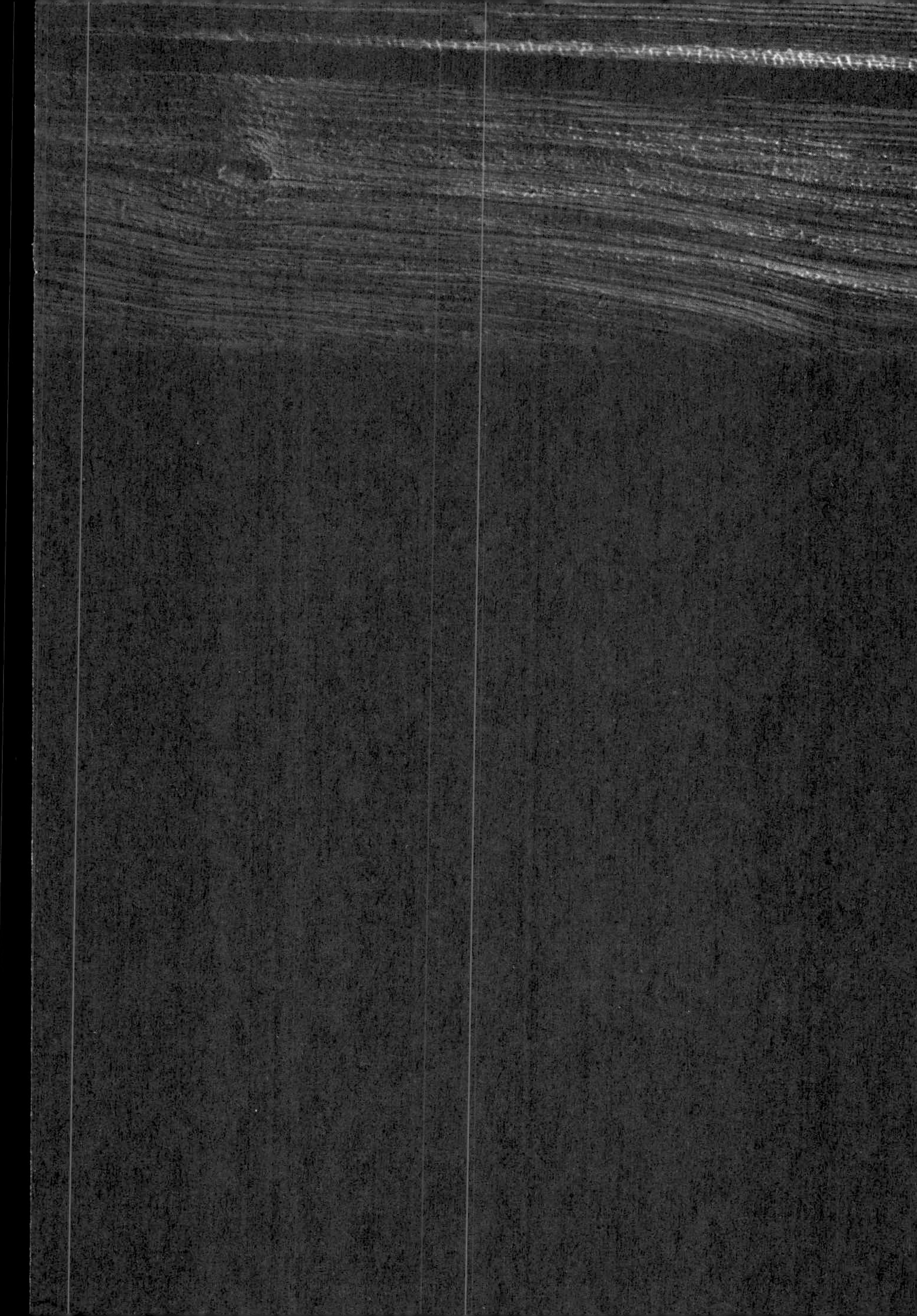

"Our Father, who art in heaven . . ." Don Joachim Rodrigo was a very pious man. His nervous fingers rolled against the worn wooden rosary that he used for everyday prayer. He was a spiritual man. He attended Mass at the old church every morning in order to start his day in the proper frame of mind. He ran his household with fatherly compassion and was known as a most scrupulous businessman. That is why, finding himself aboard a sea vessel weighted down with humanity, Don Joachim Rodrigo found himself terribly ill at ease.

He shuddered at the possibility of his beloved wife discovering his true whereabouts, for she, beyond any doubt, was a good and just woman.

"Hallowed be Thy name . . . I am lower than the serpent!" His lips twisted the words of the familiar adoration. He tightened his grip on the bead and stared out across the white foam whipping up pointy tips on the rolling green ocean. His stomach began to churn along with the waters. But Don Joachim knew that his misery was superficial. Even as he felt his muscles tighten in sudden spasm, he knew that below him—only a few feet beneath his calfskin boots—were creatures in deep and true pain.

"Thy will be done . . ." Don Joachim tried to shut his ears against the low moans issuing up from the hold. "Forgive us our debts . . ." He could not go on. His hands shook so that the rosary clattered to the deck. He stooped to recover them, and a sturdy wind lifted the putrid smell up through the wooden planks. Don Joachim's fifty-five-year-old knees buckled. He smelled sweat and tears, and waste and fear.

"Christ, mate! Hold it together, then!" A rough hand jerked Don Joachim up and shoved him inside his cabin. The tight, airless space served only to trap the odors surging through his nostrils and into his brain. The sailor slammed the door, leaving Don Joachim slumped against the swaying wall.

Everything had begun, truly innocently, one month ago. It had only been a matter of business! At that time, Don Joachim was satisfied in his prosperity. He found joy in his only daughter, Rosalinda. And he took pleasure in the promise of his sons, Claudio, Benito, and Manolo. Indeed, his greatest pleasure was in his eldest, Manolo. The one who counted before he could walk. The one who had learned to bargain with his brothers for their sweets. The one who slept all night in the warehouse on one occasion simply because he liked the stacks of cargo.

It was Manolo who had persuaded Don Joachim to take to the sea again for "a matter of good business." Manolo had leaned his impeccable linen sleeves across Don Joachim's document-strewn table and said, "Father, the New World is still open to those who will take a risk!" Manolo's sea-blue eyes glistened with excitement. He stepped back and smiled, letting his long hands fall open against the sturdy leather of his riding trousers.

In the six years that he had worked for his father, Manolo had developed an excellent reputation for spotting new and lucrative business opportunities. In that fact, Don Joachim could see a bit of himself long ago, hungry for a chance to prove that he could succeed. He had. Don Joachim's efforts had even surpassed his own father's, who was of noble birth but had been content to live off the income from his lands.

Young Joachim had wanderlust. He had followed a family friend to the East and found wonder and fortune there. Joachim Rodrigo became a true man of the world, embracing new languages and building a respect for cultures and habits strange to him. He used the inheritance from his father to first buy silks and rugs, then exotic hides and gleaming ivories. Some he sold right off the boat, in his province. Others he loaded again onto ships headed for the isles of the north.

In time, he sailed himself to England and France and traveled even as far as Vienna to meet his best customers, to see firsthand the luxurious robes and fine carvings they'd made from his skins and bones. The early years had been hard on Filomena. Yet she remained loyal and waited to become his wife, waited to bear and raise his children.

Now they could reap the rewards of Don Joachim's diligence, of Filomena's nights alone. He could enjoy his entire family's company often, and in leisure, while Manolo looked after their future prosperity.

Don Joachim had enthusiastically agreed with his son's proposal to test the venture beginning even farther away than Persia.

"Azúcar," Manolo had let the word roll from his tongue. Sugar plantations, he said, would spread across the lands of the New World. Someone must own them. Someone must pay the managers and overseers. Someone must transport the bounteous results of the investment back to civilization. That someone must, of course, be knowledgeable of the business world. Manolo had convinced Don Joachim. They would extend their dealings to Benezvela.

Manolo had planned it; Manolo had researched everything. He had so looked forward to this first trip to the new continent! And now a last-minute conflict over an important shipment in the Port of Cadis had interfered. Manolo would have to attend to that.

Don Joachim had decided this was the doorway to his retirement. He would make this one last and long journey to bless Manolo's rise to full partner in the family business. He would finalize the deal, perhaps by going further than expected and purchasing one of these plantations fully. Don Joachim was capable of looking both backward and forward at the same time. Manolo would have, must have a future on his own terms. He had chosen his way.

"Tell me," Joachim Rodrigo had said, "How do they keep the cost of the labor so very low?"

Manolo was hurrying into his traveling cloak with one eye on the groom and waiting horses as he thrust the contracts into his father's arms. Manolo looked to his father, flushed with momentary anxiety over all that lay on his shoulders. When their eyes met, however, he was immediately calmed by Joachim Rodrigo's reassuring smile. He hugged his father tightly, quickly. His shoulders relaxed. He opened the door with a bounce in his step. Over one broad shoulder he said, "Slaves, Father. My contact says relying on the native labor will not at all suffice. Everything is there in my notes—I must go!" The heavy door shut between them.

Slaves. It was not Don Joachim's first uneasiness with the practice.

Though he had developed a specialty in his business,

he knew that a successful man must be ever aware of current affairs, of happenings near and far. So he often shared wine and stories with many kinds of men, young and old. He knew the Portuguese were literally carving their way into the jungles of Brasil, establishing gold mines to the envy of their Spanish competitors. Joachim Rodrigo's fellow Spaniards were pushing themselves into neighboring Benezvela, boldly clearing and planting these vast plantations. Jealousy fueled the dueling nations. Unexpectedly, Spain had found a way to gain the upper hand.

Benezvelan natives, unused to the brutality of toiling a crop such as sugar, proved useless. Don Joachim's enterprising countrymen discovered that Black Africans filled the void. They could survive, even thrive in the jungle harshness.

Slaves.

Joachim Rodrigo had never seen a Moor up close. In the markets of Persia, he had seen from a distance the strapping bodies towering over the crowds, like shadows moving at will. But these had been merchants too, bargaining in many of the same languages Don Joachim himself employed in his trade. Surely, a man who could support himself thus would never fall into such a state as bondage!

And yet, in taverns and drawing rooms alike, any New World conversation seemed to turn on a different type of Negro than those Joachim Rodrigo had glimpsed. It was said that these were savage, bestial creatures from the innermost regions of the Dark Continent. Unlike the clever yellow men of the East and apparently different from the natives of the New World, these creatures were said to be unworthy of comparison with a White man from any walk of life.

The talk buzzed around and inside Don Joachim's head for a time, then hid itself from his daily routines—why would it be otherwise?—until he heard the Word read in a quavering voice by the old Padre.

> . . . Bring back my sons from
> afar, and my daughters
> from the ends of the earth:
> everyone who is named as
> mine, whom I created for my
> glory, whom I formed
> and made . . .

Don Joachim Rodrigo could recall no instance in his boyhood lessons from priests and brothers in which it was revealed that God had created man, woman, and slave.

~

Don Joachim set out two days after his son. Doña Filomena fussed over him, saying over and over that she had dreamed of black crows and begging him to leave it for Manolo. But he would not allow her to interpret the dream over café con leche and fresh bread. She accompanied him to Mass that morning and then kissed him as long and as sweetly as she had before every voyage.

He savored the taste of her well past the Islas de Canarias. He read Manolo's meticulous figures describing the five-year outlay of funds needed for the project, with earnings increasing each year.

Don Joachim Rodrigo was pleased that his son was not shortsighted.

And when Don Joachim saw the rocky coast of Africa in the distance, he felt again the familiar surge of excitement and adventure. He would go ashore, perhaps find some small but sentimental exotic trinket for Rosalinda. He saw rising toward heaven the stone walls of the Portuguese fortress on the coast.

The captain, a surprisingly well-mannered English, explained that they would stop on the mainland to pick up crucial supplies and cargo. Manolo had booked passage knowing the *Santa Clara* would be fast; it merely carried documents and foodstuffs from Spain to its settlements in Benezvela. Though the boat was small, it was traveling surprisingly light to Don Joachim's feel; perhaps there was African ivory or palm oil to be loaded here along with the crew's necessities.

He stood with the other two passengers on the deck as the crew lowered the rowboats into the water. One man, a gentleman, seemingly a man of business like Joachim Rodrigo, kept to himself. He shared nothing, solicited nothing. The other, a young cartographer, had been busy with his instruments, scrolls, and eyeglasses thus far. He proudly tilted one of his maps so that Joachim Rodrigo could see.

"I look forward to seeing some of the infamous beasts of Africa," the young man confided in Don Joachim.

"You are disembarking here, then?"

"Oh, yes!" The younger man spoke breathlessly, shoving his tools into a large satchel. He dropped something; Don Joachim bent to retrieve it for him. The other gentleman moved away from them with an air of patient impatience.

In the midst of the noise of commerce, Joachim Rodrigo felt a rush. He was expectant, eager. Why, he wondered? What did he hope for at this place? He followed the cartographer through the gates. This was a man's place, swirling with gruff shouts and clattering horses' hooves.

And then Don Joachim heard the anguished wail of a woman. He turned on his heel, ready to intercede, to offer of himself whatever was necessary to help.

But he realized, with a jolt to his heart, that he could not help this woman. She lay sprawled in shameful nakedness, fettered and bound. Her head, a mass of black twists dotted with shells and beads, was lowered against her dusky skin. She slowly raised tearless eyes. Empty eyes.

Slaves.

Joachim Rodrigo's fellow passenger—the gentleman—had gone directly toward her, pulling her chin up with one gloved hand and stretching her lips back with the other, apparently examining her teeth.

Joachim Rodrigo averted his eyes; a woman was a woman. He could not save her, but he could not witness her degradation, either. With a sinking stomach it came to him, as he blinked away, that there was nowhere to look.

For there ahead was a row of black bodies—a dozen men, with hands bound and legs spread for display. To one side were twenty more, on the other a line of women clad only in ragged skirts. Joachim Rodrigo was dizzied by the variety of expressions on the African faces.

Fearful, defiant, numbed. Haughty, clever, calculating. Regal. Intelligent. Mad. Their bodies were all submissive, but their faces! Joachim Rodrigo could see the world in their faces.

The English captain was strolling past one group of the Africans with a stout Portuguese who spoke with his hands. The English paused to pull notes from his waistcoat. A matter of business.

Don Joachim was overcome.

He stumbled somewhere, anywhere, to quiet the uncertainties vying for his conscience. He wandered into the dimness of a low wooden building.

"African heat. It is unlike our own." His counterpart from the ship—a true compatriot in all, it now appeared—offered him a drink from a bejeweled silver traveling flask.

Don Joachim knew it would be foolish, even dangerous, to partake of spirits in a heat such as this. He declined with a shake of his head and lowered himself to a rough stool. He would take no water here, either. In his present state, nothing would ease his distress.

The slaves had faces.

"Your first purchase? It is hard to believe, I know, that such savages walk on two legs and mate just as we. But they are not like us. Heathens, too—our good king says we should convert them from their wretched animal worship to our true faith."

Don Joachim blinked up as the man went on.

"It is almost a wasted effort. Our God has left these ignorant creatures where they belong, in the darkness—" The man paused in his discourse. "You are ill." The gentleman assisted Don Joachim to his feet.

"I am not," Don Joachim answered as firmly as he could. At the hearing of his voice, the man believed his lie and let him be. Joachim Rodrigo made his way out alone. The oppressive atmosphere seemed heavier inside the walls than without.

He closed his eyes and saw those faces again. Had the heat deluded him? Or had he somehow seen, at the same time, the faces of the old Padre, of the publican he once met in England, his friend Don Felipe, even Manolo? All black- and mahogany- and coffee-skinned. And as each of his friends and family and acquaintances had lives, where were the lives of these Africans? They had not sprung up from black African soil alone, each to exist with no support, no feeling from or for another. Are we, Don Joachim wondered, greater than God, in removing them and using them so?

He must go back. Back to the ship now, then back to Doña Filomena and Rosalinda. Back to Manolo to confer, to explain . . . what?

Uneasiness weighted his shoulders. He felt old, too old to have such a struggle within.

Don Joachim waited to reboard the *Santa Clara*. Ahead of him the English captain was watching his Africans march out to the rowboats.

Joachim Rodrigo was drawn to the water. He went so close that the lingering waves lapped at his boots. He did not notice. The first group of slaves was pulled reluctantly to a boat and put into it; they were unable to help themselves with both their hands and feet restrained. The captain waved them off. Next a group of men and women were separated at the water's edge.

The woman who had cried out was among them. She held herself near, very near, a slim young man with a completely bald head. The sun bounced off his crown. She arched her body to rub against him; they mouthed words that no one could hear. A sailor dragged them apart. They stared at each other, drinking each other in.

Don Joachim tasted Doña Filomena again.

The men were forced into the boat. The two crewmen rowed sluggishly; several of the Africans were very large. They were more than halfway across the deepening waters when the slim African looked back, not at his woman, but at Joachim Rodrigo.

He was sure he did not imagine it. The African locked

eyes with him. Don Joachim could see the passion and the love. He could see the anger and humiliation. He could see that the man inside the African refused to be diminished. When the slim African was done pouring his being into Don Joachim, he let out a shout and was suddenly, amazingly, standing full tall on the port side. One of the big ones rose up, then another. The three leaped over the side, carrying all the others with them.

"Man overboard!"

"Overboard!" The crewmen on the ship as well as the two in the rowboat became frantic. On shore, the captain paced back and forth but did not raise his voice.

As the heavy Africans seemed to will themselves to remain underwater, there was nothing to be done. The crewmen, diving to exhaustion, could not rescue them. The Africans had no desire to be rescued.

On shore, the woman with shells in her hair began to chant the same sound, or words, over and over. They were as unintelligible as her last words to her lover. She stomped her feet in the sand and chanted, and shook herself and chanted, and fell onto the ground, convulsing and chanting. She pulled down the woman next to her, but the others remained standing.

The English captain himself ran to her, slapping her, shaking her. Her chanting reached a feverish rhythm and then stopped.

Don Joachim saw that the captain's face held a brief, strange expression.

"Cut her away!" he called out to no one in particular. "She is dead."

"A matter of good business, that. Those two would have made great trouble." The gentleman was in his ear again.

That was when Joachim Rodrigo wondered if the gentleman was his demon.

He found no peace inside his compartment on the *Santa Clara*, and even repeating the rosary a second and third time did not hush the taunts of his conscience. Hours after the merciless seaman had shut him in and gone away, there was an impatient rapping, then banging with fists, on his door. Don Joachim blinked and swallowed back the bile that kept rising in his throat as the boat rocked. It had been a long time since he'd sailed. There were other noises, loud and destructive.

"Don Joachim!" The English captain burst in, sword drawn, panting, with bright burning eyes. "We are under attack. Come above and defend yourself, or you may be slain in your bed!"

Joachim Rodrigo slipped his rosary inside his clothing and touched the cool pearl handle of a dagger. He had purchased it in a foreign alley when Manolo was just learning to chew solid food. He had decided back then that his best defense was a calm, practical demeanor; no weapons drawn unless absolutely necessary.

His modest dress would conceal him from ransom seekers. Don Joachim always wore plain, dark woolens, and his only ornament was a small gold ring, which also served as his seal.

In all his experience, Don Joachim had faced peril; early on he had even lost some goods due to his own youthful incompetence. But he had always escaped capture. He straightened himself and stepped warily through the splintered remains of the door. He showed no fear, nor did he have any.

The deck was rumbling with confusion. Don Joachim Rodrigo inched his body along the wall, heading for the stern. Surrounding him were the grunts and thuds of hand-to-hand battle. And there was commotion below also. Shrieks and shouts. Chains dragging . . . Joachim finally peered around a huge cask on the starboard side.

"Clean house! We keep nothin' to slow us down, nothin' that won't bring profit!" A huge, dirty-faced Englishman stomped across the bridge above him, bellowing orders. Joachim Rodrigo stood still.

The original crew had been overcome. He saw two of their number already bound and prostrate just ahead. Swarming about, throwing open doors and prying loose the tops of crates, were an assortment of hungry-faced men. One of them turned.

There was a splashing near the bow.

Don Joachim Rodrigo saw two of the pirates lifting . . . a black body was hoisted up and overboard.

There was another splash.

"I want full account of all the cargo!" the imposter captain growled from above.

Don Joachim was grabbed with great force, his arms wrenched behind his back so quickly that there was no time for either the dagger or the rosary. He was hit on the back of his head. His teeth rattled in the sharp flash of pain. The old Padre's voice whispered to him:

For the sake of profit many
sin, and the struggle for wealth
blinds the eyes . . .

Then Don Joachim Rodrigo saw nothing.

He awoke after the attack with a pain behind his eyes. He remembered being struck . . . He was propped up inside the cabin, smelling the pirate captain who sat in front of him. When the pirate smiled, a hole gaped where his left front tooth should be.

Here was the devil again. Did demons have teeth? Joachim Rodrigo felt fingers of pain pressing against his temples. A haze seemed to fill the small space. Images tumbled in his mind. Black crows flying over blue waters. Doña Filomena, rubbing her body against him . . . And he was certain that God was calling, calling out to him. He heard shouts and fighting . . . but why was the old Padre hitting him?

No. It must be a dream. A fevered brain . . .

"No," Don Joachim said aloud. The pirate laughed at him.

"Blimey, you've addled his senses, Crighton!"

Don Joachim's head still hurt him terribly, but slowly his mind cleared.

"I am quite sensible," he finally said. "What has happened to the previous captain?"

The new captain rolled his eyes and leaned in until he was offensive.

"What do you think? Same'll happen to you, lest you tell me why I ought spare yer life. Travelin' spartan-like, but yer ain't no man of the cloth. Them don't carry silver daggers." He held up Don Joachim's property, tilting and turning it in the candlelight.

"Got money somewhere, y'do, or somebody's got it for yer. Tell it, then!"

The words came to Don Joachim instantly, words that were not his own. He spoke with confidence: "The Lord has anointed me. He has sent me to proclaim liberty to the captives . . ."

"What?" The pirate captain shook with laughter. "Maybe 'e is a man of God! Either way, lock 'im up with the darkies 'til we figure out what 'e's worth!"

Joachim Rodrigo was at that moment seized by an emotion unlike any he had felt before. Everything he had known and been fell away, leaving him hanging only by the Word of God.

He lunged for his dagger and twisted it against the pirate's forearm, carving a bleeding quarter moon. The man backhanded him across the tiny room. Joachim and the stool bounced off the wall; he slid down, and the stool splintered.

The captain laughed, stanching the trickle of blood on his arm with a dirty kerchief. He laughed hard and then narrowed his eyes.

"Yer ain't worth as much as that, priest. I'll ransom yer if I can, kill yer if I can't." He nodded to the crewman. "Haul 'im out to the stern and shackle 'im with his *captives*."

On the deck, Don Joachim Rodrigo could feel the constant salt mist cover his body like another layer of skin. It stung the bruise at the back of his head. The leg iron clanged shut.

Joachim Rodrigo had never used violence to settle any argument. He was shaken to his core, confused over how he dared to grab for the knife. But the insult! The insult to his faith! And the insult to the slim young African man, who would have done such a thing, and more! For he *was* a man.

And more than anything, Don Joachim Rodrigo was deeply saddened that a man had taken his own life, lost his soul, rather than submit to this enslavement. There was the tragedy and truth of it.

It was a matter of souls.

He shivered and pulled his cloak closer around himself. He wanted to pray, but he could not. The aching in his head and neck seeped into his shoulders first. In time, the aching consumed his entire body, and he could not identify its source. He was extremely tired. He shivered cold and then flushed hot, then cold again. Was it night? He heard the sound of chains settling wearily against wood.

"We . . . are . . . all . . . dead." An odd voice dropped the words, one at a time. The voice spoke in French. No, perhaps it was Arabic . . .

Don Joachim let his eyes close, clasping his beads. Now he knew: the slaves had faces. The slaves had souls. And he must let Manolo know. Where was God?

It is your crimes that separate
you from your God, it is
your sins that make Him hide
His face so that he will not
hear you . . .

Joachim Rodrigo lay in the clouds, no longer sickened by rolling seas. He was in a still place. Heaven.

"No worry."

A gentle voice with strange cadence sang near him. He opened his eyes. He was not in the hereafter, but resting upon white sheets and surrounded by white hangings. He had no strength to move his heavy limbs.

A dark spot appeared.

Don Joachim's weakened eyes fluttered. It was a hand, sweeping back the mosquito netting on the bed. He sensed a woman, but he had no strength to be anxious as the black hand came nearer, attached to a like arm and torso and face.

Don Joachim was soon able to see her eyes, and he was stricken by them. They answered his gaze; they were clear, and deep, and full of compassion.

In her closeness, Don Joachim smelled sweat and spice. The hot, soul-wrenching sands of the African coast floated past his present. His head was gripped by a sudden pain so great that he thought he must die.

She pulled away, and Don Joachim Rodrigo was afraid to be alone. He groped for her with his fingers, his heart racing. Then her shadow covered him again, sweet wine touched his lips. He tried to take the drink, feeling its warmth soak into him. His muscles eased.

He willed himself to stare upon his benefactor, trying to see beyond her face.

"No worry." She bathed his brow with cool water. "Rest," she said.

Rest. But he could not rest from disturbing dreams of Manolo in chains, of pure Rosalinda wrenched away from her brother, of Manolo diving perfectly over the side of a treacherous rowboat, of Manolo sinking slowly into blue-black waves.

Joachim Rodrigo moaned for his loss.

In time, though he knew not the measure, Don

Joachim Rodrigo's brown nurse disappeared. Other voices buzzed around him.

"He has lost his mind," someone was whispering. Don Joachim was awake, though he could not discern who was speaking beyond the white curtains.

"The injury to his head, I fear it may have grave consequences . . ."

"But can he be moved?" Don Joachim thought he recognized that one. It was . . . the gentleman from the ship, from the African shore, wasn't it? And to whom did he speak? A physician. . . ?

"Perhaps, but a long voyage . . ." The physician took no responsibility in his tentative murmuring.

"I have sent letters!" The gentleman was urgent. "He is a man of wealth; he will be ransomed. I have paid it already. He must return to Spain alive. I cannot lose my investment!"

Joachim Rodrigo breathed deeply and slowly. He parted his lips, yet in his weakness could not speak out on his own behalf. It made no difference, he thought.

He was chattel to this man, to this stranger. What was important was that he might return to those he loved, to those who loved him. Details made no difference.

He could return.

Don Joachim's mind wandered back to those sick and dying wretches in the hold of the ship, those lovers held separate on the sands of Africa by irons, and to his nurse here, who cared for him in his illness as if he were her own—none of them could go back.

Later, as the gentle black hands shaved him and fed him and turned him, he understood that he was the receiver of more than he had ever in his life given.

Don Joachim Rodrigo spent the following days giving up command of his body, for he realized it would never be robust again. He could barely croak; no words would come when he wished. He found his vision slow to mend, and even growing dimmer. His mind, however, became sharper. The course he must pursue became clearer.

Joachim Rodrigo began to understand that the New World, and all its beguiling lures, was of no consequence to his future. The loss of this venture might ruin the business. Manolo would be tested to his limits. But that made no difference. The sum of his ransom could likewise leave their fortunes in a very precarious position. He worried for Doña Filomena and Rosalinda, but what was the worth of one man? Nothing, and everything . . .

One day, strong hands lifted Don Joachim Rodrigo onto a swaying pallet and carried him to a coach. He kept his eyes closed in the extreme intensity of the exotic air; the Benezvelan sun caused his body great discomfort. He longed to be at home.

Don Joachim was carried aboard a sailing vessel, though no one spoke to him of the arrangement. The gentleman with no name had apparently seen to everything.

What could he do, in his condition, except submit?

On the voyage back, there were spacious quarters alone. He lay, wrapped in quiet feebleness and considerate warmth, ever praying. Meals were brought to him, though he barely consumed them. His hands shook, and he crept around the cabin once each day, clinging to the walls.

All the while his mind strengthened even more. Determination kept him going. How was he to do it? How was he to prove to his kinsmen the truth that he had seen with his own eyes? He must convince them that their notions were wrong, their judgments unfounded. How would he prove what he now knew with his own heart?

Don Joachim Rodrigo kept praying and receiving no answer.

And weeks later, when Joachim Rodrigo tentatively stepped onto the firmness of Spanish soil, his legs trembled. The world seemed to be made of so many colors! He could hardly bear it. The sky was brilliant blue, the sails were so white! He breathed the scent of olives.

He knew that they were all there before him, faces shining with love. He could not move for a moment, weakened by the magnificence of God's return to him. Or had he returned to God?

Manolo rushed to support him on one side, kissing him, speaking in low tones that Don Joachim did not fully understand. He smiled. He knew there was time, the right time, to tell Manolo that Benezvela might fill his coffers, but would surely drain his accounts in Heaven.

Claudio was as quickly on Joachim's other side. Don

Joachim leaned heavily against his son's shoulder, shutting his aching eyes against the strong sun. He did not see, but he could feel the crinkle of Rosalinda's silks as she embraced him. He did not see, but he could smell . . . oh, he could smell! . . . the sweetness of his beloved Filomena's perfumed breasts as she enveloped him.

And when he reopened his eyes, Don Joachim Rodrigo could see nothing earthly at all. Forever after, he could see only souls. Each that he encountered, he saw as it must have been born: as a beautiful and amazing and perfect breath of God.

# Acknowledgments

My cousin Ruth had a saying: "If it's on you, tell it." Meaning, if something is always on your mind, or heavy on your heart, speak on it. What's constantly on my mind are the questions of who we all are and why we humans are thrown together in these crazy ways, with the pains and joys and fears and triumphs that we have. I've truly come to believe that, when stripped bare, humanity is really a matter of souls.

So I'm telling you the stories of people who love and want to be loved; who have faith, lose it, and sometimes find it again. They hope and long and fight and dream for particular kinds of freedom that we today may have forgotten. As separated, segregated, distanced as we may appear to be by time or experience, I'm telling you that our souls remain connected. Our souls remain alive, always and everywhere.

Without my connections to these people, I would never have trusted myself: Austin, Mommie, Matthew, Bobbie, Mary Jack, Danah, Sharon, Sally, Hector, Deryck, Carol, Wise Andrew. And thanks to everyone else who listened to ideas, read, or has otherwise been bombarded by the details of this collection.

Jill, you deserve a stand-alone shout-out.

# About the Author

Denise Lewis Patrick was born in Natchitoches, Louisiana. She attended local schools and earned a degree in journalism from Northwestern State University of Louisiana in 1977. That same year, she moved to New York City. She has been both a writer and editor in various areas of the publishing industry, particularly for children. Denise has published more than thirty-five picture books, biographies, and historical novels for young readers.

In addition to being a published author, Denise is an adjunct professor of writing at a local college. She has also worked with budding writers in an after-school program, and has managed middle and high school writing programs.